"You're in a cabin now. You were snowbound—half-frozen before I found you."

She blinked at the man above her. He seemed to fill the room with his huge shoulders and shaggy head. "You—found me?"

A scarlet flush stung her cheeks as she realized the coarse fabric of his coat was touching her bare skin.

"I thought I'd best thaw you out. So I took it upon myself to disrobe you."

"How dare you!" Her eyes were wide with distress.

"Relax, my dear. Your virtue wasn't disturbed. I thought I'd reserve that prospect for a time when your body is warm and responsive."

"That time will never come!"

"Sooner or later it will," he said quietly.

PATTI BECKMAN's
interesting locales and spirited characters will thoroughly delight her audience. She lives with her husband, Charles, and their young daughter, along the Gulf Coast of Texas.

Dear Reader:

At Silhouette we try to publish books with you, our reader, in mind, and we're always trying to think of something new. We're very pleased to announce the creation of Silhouette First Love, a new line of contemporary romances written by the very finest young adult writers especially for our twelve-to-sixteen-year-old readers. First Love has many of the same elements you've enjoyed in Silhouette Romances—love stories, happy endings and the same attention to detail and description—but features heroines and situations with which our younger readers can more easily identify.

First Love from Silhouette will be available in bookstores this October. We will introduce First Love with six books, and each month thereafter we'll bring you two new First Love romances.

We welcome any suggestions or comments, and I invite you to write to us at the address below.

Karen Solem
Editor-in-Chief
Silhouette Books
P.O. Box 769
New York, N.Y. 10019

PATTI BECKMAN
Love's Treacherous Journey

Silhouette Romance

Published by Silhouette Books New York

America's Publisher of Contemporary Romance

Other Silhouette Romances by Patti Beckman

Captive Heart
The Beachcomber
Louisiana Lady
Angry Lover

SILHOUETTE BOOKS, a Simon & Schuster Division of
GULF & WESTERN CORPORATION
1230 Avenue of the Americas, New York, N.Y. 10020

Copyright © 1981 by Patti Beckman

Distributed by Pocket Books

ISBN: 0-671-57096-X

First Silhouette printing August, 1981

10 9 8 7 6 5 4 3 2 1

America's Publisher of Contemporary Romance

Printed in the U.S.A.

Love's Treacherous Journey

Chapter One

"But I despise that man, Mike. I don't want to get within a hundred miles of him!"

Katy O'Hara's blue eyes snapped. The sprinkling of brown freckles across her Irish pug nose was accented against the angry paleness of her face. She glared across the desk at her boss.

Mike Dale, editor-in-chief of *Personality Magazine* looked at his junior editor with mild amusement. "How could you despise him, Katy? You've never met the man."

"I know him by reputation," she retorted. "He's conceited, ruthless and self-centered. And something else—" she broke off, on the verge of blurting out personal information that she impulsively decided should be kept private.

Dale shrugged. "Craig Sverenson might be conceited. Lord knows, he has enough to be conceited about. He's lived the kind of life other men read about in adventure stories. I'll admit he has something of a reputation as a lady killer. Is that what bothers you?"

Katy felt her cheeks grow warm. "It doesn't exactly endear him to me. I hear he's had romantic flings with women ranging from secretaries to movie stars." *And one closer to home,* she added to herself grimly.

Dale chuckled, waving his hand with a gesture of impatience. "Katy, you're in the publishing business. You know how fan magazines exaggerate things like that. But even if some of it is true, what difference does it make? I'm not asking you to have a love affair with the man. I just want a good firsthand story about him."

Katy sighed. "I know that, Dale. And I don't mean to sound so self-righteous, or so prejudiced. It's just that I'd be uncomfortable being around him, talking with him, writing about him. I couldn't do an objective piece. I'd have my mind made up about him before I wrote a word."

"Well, first of all I wouldn't want you to be all that objective, Katy. That's why I want you to do the piece. Your writing always has a personal, subjective, emotional tone that our readers like. And I'm not that worried about your being unfair or prejudiced in reporting about him. You have too much integrity as a writer. You'll wind up being fair no matter what kind of preconceived notions you may have about your subject."

Dale paused to grope under the mass of papers on his cluttered desk. After a diligent search, he found a battered pipe, filled it with tobacco from a can in his desk drawer, got it lit and settled back in his swivel chair, gazing at Katy through a cloud of smoke. "Craig Sverenson," he continued, "is a rare commodity, a red-blooded dashing hero. And people need to read about heroes these days. Sverenson is bigger-than-life.

He's a throwback to the days of explorers who set out on expeditions across uncharted seas in creaky sailboats with mutinous crews. He reminds movie fans of the he-man stars of the thirties and forties . . . Gable, Bogart, Cagney. He's always making headlines with some new adventure—skin-diving in the Caribbean after sunken treasure, flying a hot-air balloon across Europe, driving a race car at Le Mans . . ."

"All carefully planned to enhance his macho image," Katy pointed out sharply. "Mike, you know as well as I, those so-called hair-raising daredevil escapades of his are publicity stunts."

The magazine editor shrugged. "Maybe."

"Sverenson is a phony," Katy persisted. "He's contrived somehow to get half the women in Europe panting after him. I don't think American women will fall for a super macho type like that."

"You may be right," Mike Dale grinned, "or you might be wrong. My hunch is that movie fans will go for a real man and I think he's going to strike the public here with the impact of a new John Wayne plus a touch of Evel Knievel. He isn't afraid to tackle anything. He has a reputation of never using a stand-in or stunt man for the dangerous scenes. Does all the risky stuff himself."

"Do you really believe that?" Katy exclaimed.

"I don't know. That's one of the things this magazine wants to find out. Now, whatever you think of the guy personally, Katy, you have to admit he's turned out some great films in Europe. They've won all kinds of honors at Cannes."

Grudgingly Katy admitted, "I'll give the devil his due."

The chief editor pawed through the papers on his desk again, and eventually located the object of his search. He sat back, scanning a paper, puffing thoughtfully on his pipe. "Now, this movie he's working on, his first American film . . . he's going to direct it as well as act in it."

"A regular Orson Welles," Kate muttered. Then she listened with a feeling of sullen rebellion as her boss outlined enthusiastically his plans for a major article about the famous Swedish movie star. "He's shooting most of the film on location. It's an outdoor adventure saga, the kind of thing he does well. Sort of modern western. The story follows the hero on a trip down the Rio Grande. He'll shoot some scenes at the headwaters of the Rio Grande in the mountains of Colorado. Some of the action will be filmed in New Mexico, some where the river winds through canyons in the Big Bend National Park and part of the story will take place in border towns in Texas. We've approached him and he's agreed to let us send a writer and photographer along on the journey. We'll make it our feature cover story and schedule it to appear shortly before the film is released."

"And I'm to be the writer who goes on this wild trip down the Rio Grande," Katy said.

"Right. It will be the biggest story you've worked on since you've been with us, Katy. I know you can do a terrific job on it."

Her blue eyes threatened to fill with tears. "Mike, I was born and raised in Manhattan. I'm a city girl. What the heck do I know about going down the river on a rubber raft? I'm scared to death of snakes. If I go to Coney Island for an hour in the summer, my freckles pop out. Once I went on a weekend trip in the Adirondacks with my Girl Scout troop. I got mosquito bitten, lost and rained on. I promised myself I'd never go any place again that didn't have indoor plumbing. How can you ask me to do this?"

He waved aside her objections impatiently. "Katy, you're a young, healthy girl. There's nothing dangerous about this trip. Good Lord, there's an entire film crew going along. Sverenson will have a whole entourage of motor homes and trucks following him along the river."

"So much for your sixteenth century explorer setting out on an uncharted sea in a leaky boat," she muttered.

"Well, this trip is quite a bit different from exploring a rain forest along the Amazon that is inhabited by head hunters," Mike Dale admitted, "which, I might add, Sverenson has done. Still, the Rio Grande does go through some primitive desert and mountainous areas. I'd like to make that trip myself. Just think of going past those canyons in the Big Bend where prehistoric cave paintings still exist!"

There was a moment's silence. Katy sighed. "Mike, I just don't want to do this assignment. Can you send someone else?"

He shook his head slowly, chewing on his pipe stem. "I don't have another staff writer to send. I suppose I could get some free-lancer to do it, but I'd prefer not to. This is such an important piece, I want to have someone I know well, someone on the staff. And it's the kind of in-depth personality thing you do so well. We don't want a travelogue about going down the Rio Grande, although of course the colorful setting will be part of the story. But mainly it will be a close-up look at the man himself, Craig Sverenson, in action. You can do that. You can penetrate the surface image of this man. American readers are eager to know what Sverenson is really like."

Mike Dale leaned forward, his shaggy eyebrows lowered over piercing eyes. "Katy, three years ago you walked into this office clutching a degree in journalism from Columbia with the ink barely dry on the sheepskin, begging for a chance to be on the staff of *Personality Magazine*. I wanted to tell you to come back after you'd had a few years' experience, but that stubborn Irish in you wouldn't take 'no' for an answer. You planted yourself in that chair and talked until I finally gave you a job to get you out of my hair. I figured you'd screw up so badly that I could fire you in about three weeks. Instead you showed us all you have a lot on the ball. You've become the most promising young member of our staff. This is your chance to do a really big front-page piece for the magazine. Don't blow this, Katy."

She chewed on his words mentally for a moment, read between the lines, then met his gaze evenly. "I think what you're saying, Mike, is that if I refuse this assignment, I'd better start looking for another job. Is that it?"

He made a defensive gesture. "I hate to sound so coldblooded but I have to answer to the publisher, Katy. If I tell him I have a junior editor who refuses to do a story because she gets freckles in the sun, he's going to have my head in a basket—"

The sound of the telephone interrupted him. He said, "Excuse me, Katy," and picked up the instrument.

While he was involved with his telephone conversation, Katy arose and moved to the office window. From this sixth floor vantage point she could look down on the wet streets of her beloved Manhattan. She saw the gleaming rain-slick yellow tops of taxicabs, the black circles of umbrellas bobbing across intersections. Raising her eyes, she took in the spires and towers of the city dissolving in the rain clouds that hung low over the skyscrapers. Drops of rain splattered against the windowpane and trickled down in tiny rivulets. In the wet surface she saw her own reflection, an oval face framed with copper hair, blue eyes, pug nose, a face as Irish as her name, not a glamorous face by any means. She'd often wondered if it could even be called pretty. But she'd been too busy with her college career and then her first job here at *Personality Magazine* to be very concerned. She hadn't had time to think a great deal about boys or dates. It had been too important for her to do something with her life. She knew what a struggle it had been for her father to send her through college on a New York policeman's salary. She had needed desperately for him to be proud of her, to make it up to him for not being the son he never had. They'd had a close, loving relationship, even closer after her mother died. He'd never made her feel she'd disappointed him because she was a daughter not a son. But she could see the half concealed envy in his eyes when his buddies on the police force bragged about their sons going to the police academy or winning at sports or becoming doctors or lawyers. So she'd made up her mind to make her Dad proud of her in the only way she could. And so far she had succeeded.

Mike finished his telephone conversation and swung his swivel chair around so he could face her. "Well, have you thought about it, Katy? What's your answer? Will you do this piece for us?"

"Oh, Mike," she sighed, "you know darn good and well you have me over a barrel. How can I say 'no'? This job is too important to me."

A smile tugged at a corner of his lips. "There are other jobs for bright young girls with your talent," he teased.

"Yes and lots of other bright young girls after them. Fat chance I'd have at another job in the publishing field if I got fired from this staff because I refused an assignment!"

Mike chuckled. "I'm not that much of a Simon Legree. I'd give you a good recommendation, Katy, you know that. But I don't want to fire you and I don't want you to quit. I simply want you to do this piece. Most young reporters would jump at something like this—a trip down one of the most interesting and colorful rivers in America with an attractive continental movie idol."

"That may be the way you see it. I see it as a murderous trek into the wilderness where I'll probably get snake-bitten or attacked by a mountain lion while in the company of a man I dislike intensely."

"You'll be well covered by company insurance," he reassured her.

"Thanks a lot," she retorted dryly. "I'll remember that when I wake up one night to find a tarantula sharing my sleeping bag." She shuddered.

"Here's something that should make you feel better," he countered. "We're sending a photographer with you, of course." His eyes twinkled. "Would you like to know who it will be?"

Again she felt her cheeks grow warm. "I—I can't imagine—"

"I bet you can't," he grinned. "Well, I thought you might feel better if Tony Wilkins goes with you. From what I hear in office scuttlebutt, you two are pretty good friends. More than good friends. Who knows, after a month together in the rugged wilderness of

Colorado and New Mexico and in those romantic border towns in Texas, you might come back wearing an engagement ring!"

Now she was blushing furiously, which made her freckles more obvious, which in turn made her even more self-conscious. "Tony and I are just good friends," she stammered.

He chuckled, obviously not believing her. Then he said, "Now here's your schedule. Craig Sverenson and his party are located in a mountain resort home in the San Juan Mountains in southern Colorado. You'll fly to Alamosa, and you'll have to rent a car there to drive up to meet Sverenson's party. Tony is finishing up a photo assignment that will take him a couple more days, so he'll follow you later this week. Stop by the bookkeeping department and get your expense money and have them make your airline reservations. I'd like for you to leave right away—tomorrow if possible."

Katy spent the remainder of the morning tying up loose ends of the work on her desk and tried not to think about the unpleasant job ahead of her. Just before she left at noon, there was a tap on her door. Tony Wilkins' touseled head appeared. "Too busy to talk?"

"Oh, Tony," she said, somehow relieved to see him. "Come in."

He sauntered into her cubicle, lowered a heavy camera bag to the floor and dropped his lanky frame in an office chair. He was wearing a cheerful grin. "I hear we're off to the wilds of Colorado on an assignment together."

She nodded grimly. "Yes and I'm not too happy about it."

He looked surprised. "Why, Katy? Sounds like a dream job to me. A month or more away from smog city, breathing all that fresh air, enjoying the scenery, romantic nights in sleeping bags under the stars—and getting paid for all that, too!"

Katy sighed. "Well, I have my reasons for not turning handsprings."

The photographer gave her a puzzled look. Then he said, "How about having dinner with me tonight so we can talk about it?"

"I'd like that," she replied, pleased that he had asked. She felt the need to talk about the situation with someone and she knew she could comfortably unload her feelings on Tony.

"We could go to that Italian place you like in the Village," he suggested.

"Sounds just fine. Want to pick me up about seven-thirty?"

"Sure." He arose and slung his camera bag over his shoulder. He looked at her fondly for a moment, suddenly bent over her desk and kissed her lightly, then winked. "See you tonight." He left the office, whistling off-key.

Katy stared at the door he'd just closed, wondering at her own feelings. She had a relaxed, comfortable relationship with Tony. She supposed they had an understanding that neither had put into words, though she'd be hard put to explain exactly what it was. She wasn't dating anyone else and didn't think Tony was either, though they'd made no commitment along those lines. Her time had been too occupied with this job to be thinking about any romantic entanglements. Six months ago, Tony had started working for *Personality Magazine*. He was a top-flight photographer, one of the best in the business. He had a relaxed, easy-going manner that camouflaged an intense dedication to his craft, but made Katy feel at ease with him. She'd liked him from the start and he'd immediately taken an interest in her. When he'd asked for a date the first time, she surprised herself with an immediate acceptance. Since then she'd gone out with him once or twice a week, hence the office gossip that they were becoming serious. Were they? As for herself, she couldn't be sure. As much as she liked Tony, she wasn't ready for a serious involvement. She didn't know if he felt the same way. Perhaps he sensed her unreadiness and so wasn't pressing matters. He seemed content for the present to keep things between them light and casual. But she sensed a need for more than that growing in him. She wasn't sure sure how she'd react when the time came that he asked more of her. Maybe that was one reason why he seemed so pleased that they would be on this assignment together. A trip away from the city and the offices of the magazine, together in a new and exciting environment, might mean a turning point in their relationship. She thought about Mike's teasing prediction that she might come back wearing an engagement ring. She blushed and slammed a desk drawer.

She grabbed a quick lunch downstairs, then rode the subway to the small East Side apartment she shared with her father. He was working an afternoon and early evening shift, so she'd have to tell him about her trip when she came back from dinner tonight.

She spent the afternoon packing, a frustrating task since she was at a loss to know how to prepare for the journey. It would start in the high Colorado mountains near the Continental Divide so she assumed that she'd better be prepared for cold weather even though it was spring. But then they'd be going into the desert where she'd need light clothing. That meant two different wardrobes jammed into as little space as possible. She selected only rough, casual wear: jeans, sweaters, mittens, shorts, shirts.

Then she muttered aloud, "Darn, I don't have any kind of hiking boots!" That meant a hurried dash back downtown for a last minute shopping trip.

She was racing around the apartment, putting the finishing touches on her make-up when the door buzzer sounded at exactly seven-thirty. She answered the intercom. "It's Carlton, the door man," said Tony's cheerful voice.

"I admire your promptness but for once I was hoping you'd be a few minutes late," Katy said breathlessly. "Come on up and you can watch me put on my lipstick."

"I'd rather help you take it off," he offered.

"Fresh!" she grinned and pressed the button that released the downstairs lock.

In the taxi going downtown Tony kept up a line of casual chatter for which Katy was grateful. She wanted time to catch her breath and collect her wits before getting into a serious discussion about the Craig Sverenson assignment.

When they were at the restaurant, after Tony had given the aproned waiter their order and they were sipping glasses of rich, heavy Chianti, Tony said, "I gathered from what you said in the office this afternoon that you are less than delighted about this assignment."

Katy nodded. "I tried to talk my way out of it, but Mike had his mind made up. You know how stubborn that man can be when he decides on something."

"I sure do. But why are you so opposed to going, Katy? I still don't understand. This sounds more like a vacation trip than work."

"I know, Tony, and most people would probably feel just that way. But first of all I'm uneasy about subjecting myself to the rigors of outdoor life. I've lived in Manhattan all my life. Riding a raft down white water and sleeping on rocks somehow doesn't awaken any sense of adventure in me. I'm afraid I don't have much of the pioneer spirit. I'm a twentieth-century urban girl. In addition to that Craig Sverenson turns me off. He may be a dashing adventurer to millions of movie and TV fans and a romantic heartthrob to starry-eyed maidens but he's a phony three dollar bill to me. I dislike the prospect of dealing with him."

Tony sipped his drink, mulling over what she had said. "Is it something personal between you and Sverenson?" he asked tentatively.

"I've never met the man if that's what you mean. Mike asked me the same thing this morning. I've seen and heard enough about him to form an opinion about him." She hesitated, then went on, "But yes, there is something else too . . . a more personal matter."

Tony raised an eyebrow in surprise but kept a discreet silence while he waited for her to continue.

"I really didn't want to go into this with Mike," she began slowly, groping for the right words. "First of all, it wouldn't have made any difference with him. He had his mind made up that I was going to do this assignment long before he called me into his office and a stick of dynamite wouldn't have budged him. If I'd brought up this personal matter he would have just brushed it aside and labeled me a silly emotional woman. Besides, I didn't feel comfortable talking with him about it. I . . . felt it was a private matter—"

She hesitated again, sorting out her feelings. She found it quite easy to confide in Tony. Perhaps that meant she cared more for him than she realized or at least their relationship had become more intimate and personal than she'd suspected. She didn't want to pursue that question any further now; she was just happy Tony was here and she had a friend she was comfortable with so she could unburden her feelings.

She began, "I had a close friend at Columbia. A lovely girl named Janet Powers. She was studying the field of visual media, particularly TV production. The summer we graduated I got this job with *Personality Magazine* and Janet landed a job with a TV crew that was going to film a documentary in Egypt. I remember how thrilled she was and how excited I was for her. I saw her off at the airport. Her eyes were sparkling, her cheeks flushed—" Katy paused, swallowed, then went on. "You can guess what I'm leading up to. The documentary was that thing on Egypt that Craig Sverenson did for public television. Being on his crew, Janet met Sverenson, of course. I don't know exactly what happened between them. Janet never spelled it out. From what I could read between the lines in her letters she'd fallen head-over-heels in love with him. I assume they had a love affair and when they finished filming the documentary Craig tossed her aside and went on to other romantic adventures. Poor Janet . . . when she came back, she looked terrible. She'd lost a lot of weight and was in a serious depression. I was scared to death she was going to gulp a handful of sleeping pills one night. I spent all the time I could with her, Tony. The poor girl was an emotional wreck. She couldn't work. She kept losing weight. But she wouldn't see a doctor. Kept saying they don't make pills for a broken heart, which I guess is true. Finally she went out to California to stay with some relatives. Eventually she pulled herself out of it. She got a job with a TV studio out there and the last I heard she was getting along pretty well again, though I suppose she'll have emotional scars all her life." Katy sighed. "Anyway, that's my personal experience with how Craig Sverenson treats women. He broke my best friend's heart and put her through hell. You can see why I dislike the man intensely, even though I've never met him in person. He's an egomaniac, and he doesn't care whom he hurts in the process of feeding his colossal ego—"

Tony listened sympathetically, nodding soberly. "Yes, I can understand your feelings, Katy. That was a rough thing to go through with your friend." He was thoughtful for a moment, then pointed out, "Of course as you say, you don't know the whole story—"

Katy agreed, "That's true. Janet never would open up about it completely. I guess it was too painful for her to talk about. But it was pretty obvious what had happened. I know Janet isn't the first person to get hurt in a romantic encounter and won't be the last. It's just that her experience, added to the other things I've heard about Craig Sverenson, has me prejudiced against the man.

"What if you are right and he is a rat?"

"Then that's what I'll tell our readers. Mike wants me to be honest."

"Good for you," Tony grinned. Then he said, "Of course I have a whole different feeling about this trip. I don't mind roughing it. Matter of fact, a buddy and I used to go backpacking during our summer vacations. This trip is going to be a photographer's dream. Y'know, Katy, however you might feel about Craig Sverenson, you have to admit the guy's got a lot on the ball when it comes to filmmaking, both in front of and behind the camera."

"Yes, I admitted that to Mike. I have to give him credit. He can act. And he's supposed to be a good director, too."

Tony went on with boyish enthusiasm. "We'll be rubbing elbows with famous movie stars and see a movie being filmed. And the location is terrific. I've read a lot about the Rio Grande. That's one reason I'm excited about this trip. The river is drenched with history. The Pueblo Indians in New Mexico built their adobe villages along the Rio Grande. Coronado searched for the seven cities of gold there. Famous outlaws, border raiders, Pancho Villa's army rode their horses across the river and turned it red with blood. We'll see alpine forests in Colorado and deserts in Texas. When the Rio Grande goes through the Big Bend, it passes between three gigantic canyons twelve hundred to fifteen hundred feet deep."

The photographer paused with a self-conscious chuckle. "I'm starting to sound like a travel agent—"

"That's all right, Tony. Keep talking. Maybe you'll convince me." She gazed at her date thoughtfully, at his mop of hair that resisted combing, his friendly brown eyes, his lanky six foot frame. She felt a wave of fondness for him. Having him along might make the trip bearable. "I'll try not to spoil this assignment for you, Tony."

"Once we get underway you'll feel different," he assured her confidently. "We're going on a fantastic adventure, Katy. You're going to love it."

"I hope you're right," she said without conviction.

Katy's father was home when she returned from her date with Tony. Big John O'Hara they called him on the police force, an apt description, Katy thought as she saw his bear-like figure reducing their kitchen table to a child's play toy. But with her he was tender and gentle. He'd been both a father and a mother to her since her mother died when she was thirteen. As far as she was concerned he'd done an admirable job.

Big John was having his favorite bedtime snack after coming in from a late shift: scrambled eggs and a cold beer.

"Been out romancin' that photographer feller agin, have ye?" the big policeman rumbled, pretending to scowl, but giving her a wink.

"Now wouldn't you like to know, John O'Hara," she retorted, a grin tugging at her lips.

"Don't give me none of your lip, girl. Now tell me, have ye broken the lad's heart yet, or are you gonna tease him a bit more first?"

She wrinkled her nose at him. Then she opened the refrigerator, poured herself a glass of milk. She sat at the kitchen table, across from her father. She felt tired and close to tears. "Dad," she said, "the magazine is sending me to Colorado on an assignment."

The big Irish cop's eyes widened for a moment and he pursed his lips thoughtfully. Finally he said, "Well, now. I'll be missin' you, girl."

"And me, you," she sighed. "But I don't have any choice. It's my job."

"Sure an' 'tis. I'm proud of what you've made of your life, Katy, darlin'. Your mom would be proud, too, you writin' for that big magazine an' all. Tell me about this here assignment in Colorado."

"Well, it will start in Colorado, but wind up in the border towns in Texas. I'll be gone a month at least, maybe longer. . . ."

She quickly explained the nature of the assignment

23

but left out her negative feelings about Craig Sverenson. She saw no reason to burden her father with her unhappiness about that part of the job. But she did admit, "I'm kind of scared about going into the wilderness like that, Dad. Part of the river goes through or near cities like Albuquerque, El Paso and Laredo. But it also goes through some of the wildest, most desolate and remote areas in the country."

"Shucks, you're a strong, healthy lass, Katy, twenty-four years old, an' able to take care of yourself," he boomed. "There'll be a whole movie crew along. It won't be no more dangerous than wandering out into some parts of this city at night alone."

"I know but I'm used to the city. I know how to take care of myself here."

"Well, I'm not worried. You'll do all right. And imagine gettin' to be right there with Craig Sverenson, makin' a movie. He's a big name these days. An' he'll sure know how to take care of you and his party. He knows all about wilderness survival."

"Yes," she muttered, keeping her emotions about Craig Sverenson to herself.

She had the feeling that she wanted her big policeman father to take her on his lap tonight and comfort her as he'd done when she was a youngster waking up crying from a nightmare. Something told her she'd be leaving her safe childhood behind forever when she got on the plane in the morning.

Her father rode to the airport with her the next day and she was grateful for his moral support. He was an irresistible optimist who could see nothing but the bright side of things. She had the feeling that he thought this trip would be good for her, a necessary step toward independence and maturity.

But when her plane took off and she looked down at the familiar granite spires of Manhattan fading behind her, she couldn't shake the dark premonition that she was walking straight into a disastrous experience.

Chapter Two

In a matter of hours she was looking down at the blinding white sand dunes of Almagorda passing beneath the plane's wing tip. And she was seeing the majestic snowcapped peaks of Colordao's San Juan mountain range.

Her plane landed at Alamosa. When she was on the ground, the dry clear air gave her spirits an unexpected lift. It was an invigorating change from the humid, muggy atmosphere of Manhattan. The temperature was cool but spring-like. When she gazed at the enormous mountain range turned blue by the distance, except for the higher elevations that were dazzling white, she felt a wave of awe unlike anything she had experienced before. She stared speechlessly at the dramatic setting. It was like being in a great outdoor cathedral built not by men and machinery but rather by the hand of God Himself. Nothing she had seen in photographs or movies had prepared her for the overwhelming impact of such rampant splendor. For this moment at least she was glad she had come. Her office back home that she had loved now seemed confined and artificial by comparison. She found her emotions confused, her senses dazzled by this staggering change in her frame of reference. Everything had expanded like a movie screen that had suddenly widened to Cinerama. It was all a little frightening and was going to take some adjustment on her part.

She felt somewhat out of touch with reality as she secured her luggage and then followed her boss's orders to rent a car. She had been given detailed instructions and a map on how to find the Sverenson camp. She would follow the main highway, 160, west out of Alamosa for a distance of some fifty miles. Then she would turn onto roads that would lead her into the Rio Grande National Forest, up into the San Juan mountains where she would be driving over passes at altitudes of 10,000 feet and more.

As she drove out of Alamosa she saw dark cloud masses piling up over the mountain ranges ahead of her. She switched on the car radio and turned the dial until she found a local station giving a weather report. A late-season Pacific cold front was moving in. But they were well into spring, she thought. She was surrounded by sunny, pleasant weather here on the plateau in a desert-like setting. Wild flowers were growing in profusion along the roadside. She couldn't believe that a cool front this late in the season would do more than drop the temperature a few degrees.

Perhaps it was the change in altitude, going from a sea level environment to the thinner oxygen in the air and reduction in atmospheric pressure. She had the sensation of being slightly intoxicated, a feeling of being "high" and not quite a part of reality.

Along the semiarid high plains grew desert-like

plants and flowers, grasses, sand begonias, various forms of cacti and yucca plants. But as she drove into the foothills in higher altitudes from 6,000 to 8,000 feet, the vegetation changed to bright red Indian paintbrush, white and pink larkspur, the purplish cup-like pasque flowers and the white, red and yellow tulip-like flowers of Mariposa.

As her rented sedan labored up steeper and steeper grades, Katy felt her ears become stuffy. She swallowed and yawned to clear them and then remembered that chewing gum sometimes helped when changing altitudes, so she popped a stick in her mouth.

The clouds that had been a distant threat when she started out from Alamosa now hovered over the very mountains she was climbing and they were like masses of dark mist settling down over the treetops. Lightning flashed in the boiling clouds and thunder rumbled. She realized she was shivering and quickly turned on the car heater. Incredulously, she saw patches of snow on the side of the road, patches that became deep drifts as she went higher into the mountains. It seemed unbelievable that an hour ago she had been in a desert-like high plains region with a spring-like temperature, and now she was passing snow drifts in an ever increasing alpine atmosphere.

She had gone from scrubby, waist-high desert cacti to towering forests of spruce, fir and aspen. The terrain around her was like a painting of brown, green and white splashed on canvas by an artist gone mad. Clear icy mountain streams raced pell mell down great chasms, over rocky beds and waterfalls, slowed here and there by ponds created by beaver dams. The wounds and scars caused by monstrous glaciers of a bygone ice age were evident everywhere in deep basins, glacial lakes and hill moraines—the debris left behind by the Pleistocene glaciers.

The impact on her senses was bewildering. And more frightening was the turbulent weather shrouding the higher elevations. An icy mist turned into a flurry of hail that rattled her car top and was quickly supplanted by clouds of swirling snow.

By now she was on a narrow, unpaved road, deep in the Rio Grande National Forest and climbing to passes that would take her above 10,000 feet. She stopped the car and consulted her map. The weather had her badly frightened now. The last thing she had expected at this time in spring was a snowstorm. But then she was totally unfamiliar with mountainous conditions.

She had a decision to make, whether to turn back or continue on to the Sverenson camp. Behind her were several hours of driving back down steep roads that would have become slippery and might be iced over or clogged with snow drifts. If her directions and map were right, she could be in the Sverenson camp within an hour if the passes ahead of her didn't fill with snow. Continuing on ahead seemed the most sensible alternative.

"I knew this trip was going to be a disaster," she muttered.

She started the car and continued her tortuous journey up the steep, winding road that was rapidly becoming obliterated by the falling snow. Her only choice was to stay between the avenue of trees and hope she didn't slip into a ditch.

She had not seen a house or a living soul for more than an hour. She felt totally alone in a wilderness as remote as the moon. What a fool she'd been to start out in the face of such threatening weather, she thought bitterly. But Mike had urged her to join the Sverenson party immediately before they began their trip down the river and became hard to locate. And being unfamiliar with late spring snowstorms in the mountains, she simply had not recognized the danger when she'd heard the weather forecast.

The falling snow grew thicker until she was totally lost in a swirling white cloud. It piled on her hood. Except for the arcs of the wipers, it was stuck to the windshield. But the wipers and defroster accomplished little, for she couldn't see past the hood of the car anyway. She couldn't see the trees any longer. Wherever she looked there was only a wall of dense snow.

She felt the car slide and shudder and heard the sickening whine of a back wheel spinning wildly with no traction and she knew she'd gone off the road. She realized with icy fear that she might be hanging on the edge of a precipice above a sheer drop of thousands of feet.

She switched off the engine, put the transmission in park and set the emergency brake. Then she huddled alone in the awful silence.

Despair more dreadful than anything she had experienced before in her life spread through her like the cold that was chilling her to the bone. Panic made it difficult for her to breathe. She thought of ghastly accounts she had read about motorists trapped in their cars, buried under giant snow drifts, their frozen bodies not found until days later.

She was stuck on a seldom used back road in a national forest wilderness. It was useless to hope that other cars would be coming this way. She fought to control her blind panic and to think rationally.

"Can't stay in the car," she reasoned. The sound of her own voice helped fight the panic, so she continued to talk aloud to herself. "That's how people get stranded and trapped. Must get into warm clothes and get outside and keep moving."

Her best chance for survival, she concluded, was to try and hike the rest of the way to the Sverenson camp. If she didn't get lost in the snowstorm she might be able to locate the camp on foot.

"If I don't freeze to death on the way," she thought grimly.

She crawled into the back seat where she'd stowed her luggage and put on her warmest sweater and hiking boots. Then she pushed the door open and stepped out into the swirling snow. The flakes stuck to her face and clothes and half blinded her. She ducked her head into the icy wind and resolutely began walking.

Her chilled body protested that her clothing wasn't heavy enough. She really wasn't prepared for this kind of weather. Her arms and legs felt numb. She swung her arms and tried to move faster to keep up her circulation but the high altitude and thin oxygen soon had her heart pounding and her lungs gasping for breath.

She had to pause to breathe and when she did, the chill in her body grew worse. She floundered on, slipping and stumbling on the icy terrain. Once a small avalanche of snow from the trees above her dumped a load of snow on her, almost burying her. She struggled out of the white mass, feeling the added misery of wet clothing and snow inside her boots soaking her already chilled feet.

The last of daylight faded, plunging the forest into inky blackness. Now she was totally lost. She bumped into trees, fell sobbing into deep snow drifts. She called for help until her throat was raw but the moaning wind shattered the sound of her voice.

Her legs weighed tons. She had grown inutterably weary. Somehow she was no longer afraid that she was going to die. She had grown too tired to care. When she stumbled and fell into a snowbank, she no longer had any fight left in her. It wasn't worth the effort to get up. The struggle for self-preservation had become too great a burden. Somehow she was no longer aware of being cold and wet. A tremendous lassitude overwhelmed her. She just wanted to go to sleep.

She felt herself sinking down, down, until conscious thought ceased to function.

At times she thought she was dreaming. She felt herself floating upward and being swept along by a strong, powerful force. Then there was a sensation of tingling in her arms and legs, a gradual return of feeling, of being deliciously warm and comfortable. So this was what it was like to die, she thought. Well it wasn't bad at all . . . in fact it was rather nice.

But a flickering light was annoying her. And then a deep voice, definitely not that of the angel Gabriel, commanded, "Here, drink this."

An arm propped her head up rudely. She tried to protest but a bottle was thrust between her lips. She choked and spluttered as fiery liquid burned all the way down her throat, then spread its warmth through her body. She gasped and found herself sitting up, looking around, wide-eyed and confused.

The flickering light was coming from a blazing fire which was also the source of the warmth she was feeling. It cast dancing shadows over her surroundings which appeared to be a small crude room.

A face was looking down at her, a dark scowling face and a pair of sea-green eyes that drilled fiercely into her.

"How are you now? Feeling better?" a man's husky voice rasped.

"I—I don't know." She tried to regain a grasp of her disoriented thoughts. "What happened? Where am I?"

"What happened is that you were half frozen and suffering from exposure. Where you are now is in a small cabin I happened to find."

She blinked at the man who was standing over her. He seemed to fill the room with his huge broad shoulders and shaggy head. His face was partly hidden in the shadows. She was aware mainly of a mass of black hair, a fierce black beard, a rugged weather-beaten countenance with skin like browned leather and those penetrating green eyes that glittered in the darkness with a luminescence of their own. He was a powerful man whose presence projected a vibrating force.

"You—you found me?" she asked.

"Yes," the huge man said with a chuckle that rumbled from his broad chest. "You were sprawled out in the snow like a half frozen kitten. Thought I'd best thaw you out."

Then, as she became increasingly aware of her surroundings and herself, Katy felt a distinct shock. She was wrapped snugly in a heavy fur coat that the man must have been wearing. And she felt the coarse fabric against her bare skin!

Wildly her gaze darted around the room and came to rest on her clothing drying in front of the roaring fire. She wasn't wearing a stitch under the coat.

A scarlet flush stung her cheeks. She felt confused and frightened. Apparently they were in some kind of crude one-room log cabin, isolated and alone. The fact that the stranger had saved her from freezing did not alter the fact that she was very much at his mercy. She was no longer afraid of freezing to death but a different kind of threat was turning her blood to ice. What did the man plan to do with her now that he had rescued her from the snow? The way those strange green eyes with their swirling flecks of brown were studying her made a chill race up her spine.

Her tongue felt dry as she whispered, "How did my clothes . . . I mean, who—" She gulped hard.

He grinned at her obvious humiliation. "Who undressed you? Well, I'm afraid I had to weigh the decision of your catching pneumonia against your being embarrassed."

She gasped, "You . . ."

He smiled and bowed. "Leaving you in those wet garments another moment would have meant a trip to the hospital for you. So I took it upon myself to disrobe you. I thought of averting my eyes but quite frankly the view was too lovely even though you were slightly blue and covered with goose bumps."

Katy wasn't sure which was stronger, her fright or her humiliation. "How dare you!"

He raised an eyebrow. "I should think you'd want to thank me."

"What—for taking advantage of my weak, unconscious state to—to—"

There was a glint of infuriating amusement in his eyes. "To what?"

Yes . . . what did happen before she regained her senses? She was breathing hard, her heart hammering, her eyes wide and filled with distress.

She realized he had enjoyed her embarrassment enough and was taking pity on her. He said, "Relax, my dear. Your virtue was not disturbed. I have, by some women, been called a cad—but not for anything so depraved as taking my pleasure with a half frozen and unconscious body—exquisite as yours is. No, I thought I would reserve that heavenly prospect for a time when your body would be warm and responsive."

Again scarlet flames licked up her throat to her cheeks. "That time will certainly never come!" she hurled back at him, feeling braver now.

He merely bowed his head in an arrogant manner. "Perhaps," he said quietly. "One can never predict the fortunes of war . . . or love."

As much as the man humiliated and angered her, she also found him intriguing. He spoke with a slight accent. There was something foreign about him, however, more than his speech. His manner was not like that of men she had known in the States. But it was even more than that, as if he not only came from another country but another time as well.

She touched her tongue to her dry lips, holding the coat tightly around her body. "You—accidentally stumbled on me in the snow?" she asked.

"Accident?" He shook the cabin's single window with a hearty laugh. "No, young lady. I was looking for you."

"Looking for me?" she asked, more bewildered than angry.

"Of course. I certainly wasn't out roaming about for pleasure in this miserable snowstorm. We were expecting you this afternoon. Your office had contacted us, saying you'd be arriving by plane today and would drive up this afternoon. I got to wondering if a New York tenderfoot might be stupid enough to come up through these passes in the face of a spring snowstorm. I decided I'd better take a run down the mountain on my snowmobile to check on you. Sure enough, I found your abandoned car. I followed your tracks. You'd wandered off the road. It was obvious you didn't have the foggiest notion where you were going. I found you half buried in a snowbank, soaked to the skin, unconscious and nearly frozen. Luckily I remembered this little cabin with some dry firewood. Probably a hunter's shack."

As he spoke, Katy stared at him, tantalized by the faint accent and something very familiar about his hair and eyes. And then with a shock that fairly took her breath away she gasped, "You're Craig Sverenson!"

"Of course," he grinned, white teeth flashing in the bristling black beard. "You didn't recognize me?" Then he tugged at the beard. "Oh, yes. This does fool people. I grew it for the part in this new story we're about to film."

The frightening ordeal and the humiliation she had been through was forgotten in a new flash of anger. She had just had a firsthand demonstration of the man's ego. He'd taken it for granted that she would recognize one so famous as himself immediately. Next he probably expected her to swoon at his feet! Well, she had news for him.

"No," she said coldly. "I did not recognize you."

He shrugged. "No matter. You know me now. And you, I presume, are Katy O'Hara from *Personality Magazine.*"

"Yes."

He smiled. "How very Irish you are. And the face to go with it—red hair, blue eyes and all. Tell me, Katy O'Hara, do you have a temper to match the red hair?"

"I might," she said, feeling annoyed. There was a bantering quality about his voice, as if he were deliberately trying to exasperate her—and succeeding!

"You're a city girl, right?" he went on.

Why did he make that sound like an insult, putting her on the defensive? "Yes," she frowned. "Why?"

"Your first trip into the mountains, no doubt."

"Why do you say that?"

"Because only a city tenderfoot would go driving into a snowstorm and wander around, asking for a case of pneumonia."

"You've already pointed out my lack of judgment," she retorted coldly. "You could have warned my office about the danger. It's supposed to be spring. How was I to know you got snowstorms this late in the season?"

"It's unusual though not impossible. I understand they can have blizzards up here as late as May."

"A fine time for somebody to tell me!"

He was looking her over in a bold way that brought another flush to her cheeks. "Why would your magazine send such a city girl on this kind of trip? We're going into some locations in pretty rugged wild country."

Anger brought Katy to her feet. She held the great coat tightly around her. Her eyes blazed. "Look, Mr. Sverenson. This trip wasn't my idea. In fact, I tried to get out of the assignment but my boss had his mind made up that I was to do the story. I'm here and I plan to do my job. I might be a tenderfoot, as you so insultingly put it, but I'm strong and healthy and I won't get in your way or slow down your trip down the river as you're making your film, if that's what's bothering you."

"I'm not so sure of that. I've already had to rescue you once and the trip hasn't even started. I may spend a great deal of time picking you out of the river or sending search parties to look for you."

She was trembling with rage. "Well, if that's how you feel, we can solve the matter very easily. I'll simply go back and tell my editor you refuse to allow me to do the story."

He grinned in a maddening way. "How do you propose to get back? The passes won't be open for several days. We're snowed in up here."

"Then I'm afraid you'll be stuck with me until I can drive the car back down, at which time I'll be happy to put a great deal of distance between us."

He appeared not to hear her. He was continuing to look at her in a way that humiliated her, yet made her heart pound in a strange fashion. As much as she despised him, there was no avoiding the impact of his masculinity. He was a rugged man, at home in the outdoors. He radiated the glow of strength and health.

"Might be fun to have you along, though, in spite of how inept you'll be," he chuckled. "You're a cute thing and I like the way your eyes shoot sparks when you're mad. A marvelous figure, too. I speak from firsthand knowledge."

Her cheeks blazed. "You can skip the inventory, Mr. Sverenson. I won't cause you any problems because I'm not going to do this story, even if I get fired."

"Well, let's not be hasty, little tenderfoot. You might feel better about it tomorrow after you've dried out and had a good meal. Meanwhile we're going to have to spend the night here together so we might as well try to get along."

"What do you mean, spend the night together!" she gasped.

He shrugged. "I brought you in here so we'd have some warmth and shelter. Have to wait until morning so I can get my bearings and get us back to the main camp."

Katy looked at him speechless, angry and dismayed.

38

Chapter Three

Again he appeared enormously amused by her discomfort.

"Why look so dismayed, Katy O'Hara?" he chuckled. "This could be a most pleasant and romantic interlude. A man and woman snowbound in a snug cabin for the night. We have a bottle of brandy and plenty of firewood to keep us warm. It's like a love scene from one of my movies. We could make the most of the situation and this romantic setting."

The way his piercing gaze roamed brazenly down her figure left no doubt as to the implication of his words.

She shuddered as a curious tingling sensation flooded her body making the cabin seem suddenly unbearably warm.

But anger quickly brushed aside the confusing sensation. "There is only one thing wrong with your little scenario, Mr. Svcrenson. You have the wrong woman. I am not interested in 'one night stands.' Especially with a man like you!"

He raised a craggy eyebrow. "Are you sure, Katy O'Hara? A lot of women might feel differently."

"Your colossal conceit is one of the things that makes me feel quite sure! Now I am tired and exhausted and if you'll excuse me, I'm going to try and get some rest."

He bowed in a mocking fashion and made a sweeping gesture toward the far side of the stone fireplace, indicating where she was to sleep.

She curled up on the floor, still swaddled in his huge overcoat, trying to find a comfortable position while keeping a wary eye on Sverenson.

The big burly man took his place on the other side of the fireplace, bracing his broad shoulders against the wall, his powerful arms crossed. In a matter of minutes his head nodded forward. He dozed comfortably in the sitting position. He appeared capable of relaxing under any kind of primitive condition.

Katy, still wide awake, stared at his shadowy figure with a feeling of confused and conflicting emotions. The curious thought flashed through her mind that he reminded her of a cave man dozing beside a campfire, ready to spring into action at a moment's notice to protect his lair. Again she sensed there was a quality about him that made him seem like a man out of another age. What had Mike Dale, her editor, said about Craig Sverenson? "He's a throwback to the days of explorers who set out on expeditions across uncharted seas in creaky sailboats with mutinous crews."

Yes, whatever angry feelings she might have about Sverenson, Katy had to agree with Mike's description. Sverenson certainly wasn't the average plastic, urban, twentieth century male she normally encountered. He was cast from a different mold. What it was she was not yet sure.

In any case she found herself drifting off to sleep with a sense of security. The presence of the big man dozing by the fire was reassuring. She felt perfectly safe in this primitive setting with Craig Sverenson on guard.

A bright shaft of sunlight awakened her. Then she became aware of a smell she never expected in this mountain shack—the aroma of hot coffee.

She sat up, looking curiously at her companion who was holding a small pot over the coals in the fireplace.

At the same moment he became aware that she was awake. "Good morning, Sleeping Beauty," he boomed in a cheerful, robust voice. "Ready for breakfast?"

"Breakfast?" she asked, feeling dazed and not entirely awake. "Where did you find coffee in this place?"

"My backpack," he explained, nodding toward a green bundle in a corner. "I never start out in a snowstorm without being prepared. I can offer you hot coffee made from instant grounds and melted snow and scrambled eggs from a dehydrated pack that taste almost but not quite as good as fresh from the hen."

"Sounds delicious," Katy said, suddenly aware that she was ravenous. She drank steaming coffee from a tin cup and wolfed down the scrambled eggs from a tin plate, using a plastic fork. She was thankful for his resourcefulness. She couldn't ever remember enjoying breakfast so much. At home, breakfast was an annoyance got out of the way with a quick cup of coffee and a half piece of toast.

"This altitude gives one an appetite," Sverenson smiled as if reading her thoughts.

When they finished he said, "I'll wash the cups and plates out in the snow while you get dressed." He went outside.

Thankful for his surprising concern for what was left

of her modesty, Katy slipped out of the big coat she had bundled up in and hurriedly donned her clothing that had dried beside the fire during the night. When he returned to the cabin she was fully dressed and was pulling on her boots.

"You'll be pleased to hear the following weather bulletin," he announced. "The snowstorm has ended and we have bright sunshine."

"Thank goodness," she exclaimed. "I hope I never have to go through an experience like that again!"

"Oh, it wasn't so bad," he said again, slipping into an amused, mocking tone that irritated her. "You can go home and tell your friends you spent the night with Craig Sverenson."

"Hardly something to be proud of," she snapped back.

He shrugged. "I still think you failed to make the most of a golden opportunity. Perhaps you'll regret it later?"

"No I won't," she said in a voice as cold as the icicles hanging from the roof outside. He was going out of his way to infuriate her again! She had awakened in a pleasant mood. Some of her antagonism toward him had softened during the breakfast they'd shared. She'd almost slipped into a companionable relationship with him. Now he was reminding her how much she hated him.

"Well," he said with a gallant air, "it's your loss—but mostly mine."

She looked at him, speechless. She was at a loss to know how to respond. The first part of his statement had been insulting, reflecting his colossal ego and conceit, and then he had confused her by ending on a note that had an air of gallantry, underscoring it with an old world bow. He further disconcerted her by kissing her hand with a European flourish. He was a maddening man!

"Now, shall we depart?" He opened the door for her.

She stared at him, trying to marshal her fragmented thought processes. Finally she got ahold of herself and marched outside.

"Can—can you get me back to my car?" she asked.

He closed the cabin door, swinging his backpack up on his massive shoulders. "Oh, it would be a waste of time at this point. If we located your car, we'd find it buried under a big drift. These spring snows melt rapidly. A few days of this sunshine and the roads will be clear again. As for our immediate prospects, what we need to do is to ride the snowmobile back to my headquarters."

"I thought you said you were lost, too," she said uneasily.

"That was last night, in the dark, in the middle of the snowstorm." He glanced up, squinting at the sun that sparkled down through the pine trees. "I've got my bearings now."

She could understand what he meant by the spring snows not lasting long. Already the sun felt warm on her face and the snow in the trees was starting to drip.

They mounted the snowmobile, Katy sitting behind Sverenson. "Put your arms around me," he instructed.

"No!" she retorted.

His big shoulders moved in a shrugging gesture. "Suit yourself."

The engine roared into life. They started off with a lurch and soon Sverenson was dodging the trees in a wild snow-scattering ride that had Katy screaming with terror and holding onto Sverenson for dear life. "You maniac!" she yelled.

He just laughed. "I see you changed your mind about putting your arms around me," he said above the roar of the motor.

"I don't have any choice!" she gasped. "I don't want to get killed."

Katy spent a terrifying hour, clinging to Sverenson for dear life on his mad race up and down slopes and between trees. Then suddenly they came to a halt at the top of a rise. Below them was a lovely valley with a clear stream bounding over a rocky bed, the sun sparkling on the fresh snow. Beside the stream was a building constructed in the design of a Swiss chalet.

"It's a new ski lodge, not entirely completed," Sverenson explained. "A good friend of mine is building it. He's letting us use it while we shoot the beginning scenes of the film up here at the headwaters of the Rio Grande."

Katy saw a number of four-wheel drive vehicles and two large motor homes parked beside the chalet. At the moment she was too weak from fright over the wild snowmobile ride to fully appreciate the beauty of the valley setting below. But she would bite her tongue before admitting to Sverenson how he had frightened her. He'd only make some kind of derisive remark about her being a weak, green tenderfoot from the city, unable to cope with his rugged life style. She had no intention of becoming the target for his insulting, patronizing barbs again!

Sverenson started the machine again and they swooped down the slope in a final breathtaking dash, coming at last to a stop beside the other parked vehicles, scattering snow in all directions.

Katy entered the building on trembling legs beside Craig. The lower floor of the ski lodge was a huge, open room dominated by a stone fireplace in the center, open all around, with a copper hood above a blazing fire to draw the smoke up through a chimney. A bar was situated at one end of the room. Rugs and lounging chairs were scattered about, making for an informal, comfortable atmosphere.

They were immediately surrounded by a small mob that greeted Craig with excited comments. Obviously the film crew had been deeply worried about Sverenson. "We've had park rangers out looking for you," one man said.

Sverenson, towering a head above all the others, simply roared with laughter. When the clamoring voices around him subsided, he introduced Katy to the film crew and actors and then launched into a description of the night's adventure. It was apparent to Katy that he relished a good tale, especially if it involved an adventure in which he was the central figure and he had a spellbound audience listening.

She felt a dozen eyes on her as the big film star described finding her in the snowbank. She realized her cheeks were growing scarlet and she wished she could hide in a crack in the floor. She was aghast at what Sverenson was going to say next. He was the type, she felt certain, to include how he had removed her soaked garments down to her skin. She felt a flash of impotent rage as she realized that he was fully aware of her consternation. He was looking straight at her with an infuriating grin. She thought if someone handed her a gun at this point she could cheerfully shoot him!

He held her in agonizing suspense by describing in lingering details the cabin they had found, how she was unconscious and suffering from exhaustion and exposure. Then, as if he had mortified her enough to his satisfaction, he went on to other details of the adventure, omitting the episode of undressing her. She was relieved but certain she would never forgive him for teasing her so cruelly.

When Craig had finished his story, which Katy noted had contained several embellishments, the group around them began talking again. She heard British, French and Scandinavian accents and she realized Sverenson's entourage had a definite cosmopolitan flavor.

"Now," said Sverenson, "we'll need a place for Miss O'Hara to bunk and all the rooms are occupied." His gaze swung around the crowd and settled on a tall, leggy girl who wore a green ski sweater and a tweed skirt. "Marsha, would you object to having a roommate?"

"Not at all." The blonde girl moved through the crowd and stood before Katy smiling. In an accent as British as crumpets and tea she said, "I'm Marsha Trident. Be happy to share my digs with you, such as they are."

Katy decided that she liked Marsha at first sight. The English girl had large brown eyes and a broad, friendly smile that seemed to say, "Take me the way you see me. I'm not hiding anything."

Craig Sverenson, meanwhile, had joined a group of men and they had their heads together in earnest conversation as they moved slowly to a distant corner of the room.

"That's the last we'll see of *him* for a while," Marsha said. "Everyone is upset by this bloody late spring snowstorm fouling up things and throwing us off schedule. Craig has to deal with a bunch of worriers." Then she added cheerily, "But that's not your problem, now is it? Come along and I'll show you where we bunk."

Marsha led the way up a flight of stairs, down a hallway and opened a door on a comfortable bedroom that contained two single beds.

"You look bushed," Marsha said sympathetically. "Bet you could do with a hot buttered rum and a bit of rest in a warm bed."

"Thanks," Katy said gratefully, sinking down on the side of one of the beds. "Nearly freezing to death was bad enough but riding on a snowmobile with Craig Sverenson driving was the final straw."

"Oh, you have my sympathy," Marsha nodded. "The man is an absolute maniac on one of those beastly things. You take your boots and coat off and stretch out there. I'll be back in a wink."

Marsha returned presently with a steaming mug. Katy sipped the pungent drink and made a face.

"You look as if you're downing a draft from the apothecary shop," Marsha grinned.

"I've never tasted hot buttered rum before," Katy admitted. "I guess it takes some getting used to. It does warm you up, though, doesn't it?"

"Yes, well don't drink too much the first time or you'll get swagged." Then she asked, "Did you lose all your luggage?"

"It's in my car under a ten foot snowdrift," Katy sighed. "I don't even have a toothbrush. Just what I'm wearing."

"Don't worry. We'll fix you up with all necessary essentials until they can dig your car out. I'm a bit tall for your size but the script girl down the hall is your size, if you need anything."

"Thanks." Katy felt close to tears from a combination of reaction to the night's harrowing events, Marsha's kindness and the potent drink that was making her tongue feel a bit thick. The gentle concern Marsha was showing her was a decided contrast to Craig Sverenson's rowdy and infuriating welcome.

Marsha lit a cigarette and sat on the other bed, leaning against the wall behind her. "So you're a magazine writer."

"A junior editor," Katy said with some surprise. "How did you know?"

"Dreadful bunch of gossips, a film crew like this. Especially when they're caged up in a blooming ski lodge. We heard yesterday that Craig was expecting you and when the snow started he took off looking for you." She giggled. "The producer had kittens when he found out Craig had gone off into the snowstorm like that. Craig's the cornerstone of this venture—he's the director and has the lead male role as well. If they lost him, the film would have to be scrapped and the producers would lose a good bit of money."

"I suppose I should be grateful to Mr. Sverenson," Katy said slowly. "He did save my life at some risk of his own, but—"

Marsha had raised an eyebrow, studying Katy with an amused expression. "*Mr.* Sverenson? You spent the night in a cabin, snowbound with Europe's most attractive man and you still call him 'Mr. Sverenson?'"

Katy blushed angrily. "I suppose my reputation is forever shot. No one will ever believe the evening was totally innocent."

"I believe you," Marsha replied, "though I must admit you may have trouble convincing anyone else."

"I suppose it doesn't matter," Katy sighed, "today's morals being what they are. But it matters to me. A great deal." She took another sip of the buttered rum. Either the flavor was improving or her taste buds were growing numb. She felt a slightly pleasant numbness all over.

"Well," Marsha said mischievously, "since you are up here on a writing assignment, you could always say your night in the cabin with Craig Sverenson was a matter of research."

Katy shot her a dirty look.

"Personality Magazine. Isn't that your publisher?"

"Yes. Do you ever read it?"

"Of course. Stories about celebs and all that. You have a British edition, you know."

Katy nodded glumly. She supposed she shouldn't drink any more of the rum. It was making her a bit woozy. And it loosened her tongue. Made her want to confide in Marsha more than she probably should, having just met the girl. But she felt like talking and Marsha was a good listener and probably knew Craig Sverenson quite well, being on his staff, and could give her some firsthand views of the actor. She wondered, with a sudden peculiar feeling, if Marsha had been involved romantically with Craig. She was, after all, an attractive young woman. Katy tried to interpret the confused mixture of feelings that swept through her at the thought of Marsha being involved with Craig but failed.

Recklessly she took another gulp of the rum. "Frankly I wasn't thrilled about this assignment. I tried to get out of it but my boss issued an ultimatum. Now that I'm here, I'm even less enthusiastic."

Marsha gave her a wry smile. "Craig give you a bad time?"

Katy frowned. "How did you know?"

"Oh, I know Craig. He can be a devil of a tease at times. And a regular pussycat at other times. A very complex and perplexing man."

49

"A vexing man," Katy said. "An infuriating egotist."

Marsha nodded thoughtfully. "Yes, I suppose he does have a healthy ego. Men like him do, don't they?"

"You know him quite well, then?" As soon as the words were out Katy wished them back. "Darn that rum," she apologized. "I had no business asking you that. I must—as you said—be getting 'swagged'. It's no business of mine what you and Craig . . . I mean—"

Marsha laughed. "Relax, Kate. I have never been to bed with Craig Sverenson, although I suppose I may, at times, have had some private fantasies along those lines. What woman in Europe hasn't? But no, I have had no romantic encounters with the man."

For some unexplainable reason Katy felt relieved.

"I do know him quite well, though," Marsha added. "I've worked on film crews that have done several of his movies. I do make-up, you see. I have even done Craig's make-up. Thousands of women would probably refuse to believe I actually take money for doing that."

They both laughed. Katy had another sip of the rum, then realized with horror that she'd just drained the last swallow. She showed Marsha the cup. "I'm gonna get swagged," she gasped.

Marsha grinned. "We won't tell anybody. After what you've been through, I'd say you deserve it."

"Yeah," Katy said and tossed the empty cup on the bed. "So you make up the great Sverenson face."

"Yes. It will probably fall to my lot to shave off that ghastly black beard. He just grew it for the first scene, you know."

Katy shrugged. "It isn't all that bad. Makes him look like a mountain man. A frontiersman. Listen, that's really a lot of propaganda about him doing his own dangerous stunts, isn't it?"

Marsha shook her head. "No, it's true. He's like

that—thrives on danger." A strange cloud passed over her face. She looked down as she rubbed out her cigarette in an ashtray on the bed beside her. "I sometimes think he has a death wish. . . ."

Katy tried to get a grasp on her fuzzy thinking. She wished now she hadn't drunk the rum. She had the feeling that Marsha was in a mood to talk, to reveal some personal insights about Craig Sverenson that she might not hear elsewhere. She hoped she'd remember what they talked about after the effects of the hot buttered rum wore off!

Katy said, "Listen, I'll tell you what my impression of Craig Sverenson is and then I'd like to hear yours. You certainly know him better than I do. I'll admit I was prejudiced against him before I ever came down here. The opinion I'd formed was that he was a self-centered egotist, fawned on by a lot of women, and a phony. Last night he didn't do a whole lot to change my mind. In fact, he made me so mad, I'm about ready to chuck this whole business, go back home and let my boss fire me."

"I smoke too much," Marsha muttered, shaking another cigarette from a crumpled pack. "I keep telling myself I'm going to quit. . . ." She made a vague, hopeless gesture.

She touched a lighted match to the cigarette, shook it out, then frowned thoughtfully through a cloud of smoke. "Well then, you want to know my impression of Craig Sverenson. Not easy to give in capsule form. I can tell you what he's like to work for. He's a hard-driving perfectionist. He's often ruthless, demanding almost more than a person can give, but demanding the same from himself. He's always fair, though. People who know him either love him or hate him. Those who love him are devoted and loyal. Those who hate him pray to God he'll break his darn fool neck on his next crazy stunt. Let me put it this way: he arouses strong feelings in people. It's not easy to be passive about a man like Craig.

"Let's see, what else do I know about him? Well, he likes to be surrounded by friends. He loves to tell tall tales about his adventures—stories that are basically true, although I suspect slightly embroidered here and there for dramatic effect. He loves parties. Gives them all the time. Thinks nothing of interrupting a shooting schedule to give a party, inviting the entire crew.

"He doesn't dissipate. He's something of a health nut, in fact. Drinks moderately, smokes not at all. Jogs for miles every day. Well, I suppose he must stay in top physical shape to lead the rugged, adventurous outdoor life he loves."

"You said something about a 'death wish'—"

Marsha frowned. "Oh, that's just a silly theory of mine. Psychological nonsense, probably. I just think that people who live dangerously the way he does do it either because they have a basic fear of death and have to keep proving to themselves they can lick it or because something deep inside may be setting them on a course of self-destruction. In Craig's case, if my curbstone analysis has any validity, it's the latter."

"But why—"

"Why the unconscious drive to self-destruction? Mind you, I'm an amateur at this psychoanalysis stuff. But something happened in Craig's life that could be the key." She hesitated. "Are you familiar with Dolores Ramon?"

"The beautiful Mexican actress? Yes—" Suddenly a light flashed in Katy's memory. "Wait a minute. Craig Sverenson was married to Dolores Ramon a few years ago—"

Marsha nodded soberly. "A very tragic marriage from Craig's standpoint. I think he loved Dolores deeply and wanted the marriage to succeed. She treated him shabbily. She was unfaithful to him. Finally she ran off with a producer. A divorce followed. Craig never talks about it to anybody, but if you were to ask me, he never got over Dolores. Craig is still carrying a torch for her. He's still grieving over the wrecked marriage. He's still in love with her. If you hear about his being involved in romantic flings, they were only an escape for him, a way of relieving the pain. And the fan magazines exaggerated those flings. Actually, he hasn't been involved with anyone romantically for some time."

Katy's mind had grown clearer as the effects of the rum drink faded. She mulled over Marsha's words with a patchwork mixture of feelings. Then she observed thoughtfully, "You said you weren't in love with Craig Sverenson. Sounds to me that anyone who can describe him the way you just did must be in love with him."

Marsha smiled wryly. "Correction. I said I have had no romantic encounters with the man. I didn't say I wasn't in love with him. I am, but not that way. He's my boss and I love him. Didn't I tell you people who knew him either loved him or hated him? Careful, Katy. If you stay around him very long, he'll have the same affect on you."

"He already has," she retorted grimly. "I hate him. And I'm not that sure I'm going to stick around. As soon as the snow melts I might take the first plane home."

Marsha arose and started to the door. At the point of leaving the room, she turned, holding the doorknob. "I'm going downstairs and let you get some rest. But I'll leave you with this thought. In case you decide to stick around, you may see some fireworks before the film is completed. Do you know who is going to play the lead female role in this movie opposite Craig?"

"No."

"Dolores Ramon. She's joining the filming expedition in Albuquerque. Think about that for a bit."

Chapter Four

Snow plows aided by the rapidly warming spring sunshine had the roads cleared by the next day. Katy's rented car was retrieved and brought up to the ski lodge. And the day after that Katy received a phone call from Tony Wilkins who had just arrived in Alamosa and was on his way to join her.

"Tony, it's good to hear your voice!" Katy exclaimed fervently.

"If I'd known you were going to be that happy, I would have come sooner," Tony chuckled. "How's the story going?"

"I don't know if there's going to be a story. Craig Sverenson is every bit as infuriating as I expected he'd be. Of course, he did save my life at considerable danger to his, so I owe him that—"

There was a moment's silence. "You know, you aren't making a whole lot of sense, Katy. What do you mean, Sverenson saved your life? Are you all right?"

"Yes, I am now, no thanks to Mother Nature. I am simply not designed to cope with the wilderness. It's a long story, Tony. I'll tell you all about it when you get here. But be careful driving up those mountain roads."

The photographer arrived the middle of that afternoon. Katy, who had been at a window watching for him, ran out to greet him. Tony stepped out his car, swept her up in a bear hug and kissed her warmly. "Hey, this is some fabulous area," he exclaimed enthusiastically. "I could hardly keep my eyes on the road for gawking at the scenery."

"It wasn't so great earlier this week," Katy said grimly. "I got lost in a snowstorm."

"Snowstorm?" Tony asked blankly, looking around at the meadow that was basking under brilliant sunshine.

Katy was wearing a light sweater and slacks. It was hard for her to believe she had nearly frozen to death a few nights ago. "Yes, a late spring snowstorm. I knew leaving the city was going to be a disaster for me. I got trapped in a snowbank, had to leave my car, wandered around in the dark like a darn fool and got lost. That was what I meant by Craig Sverenson rescuing me. He came down from the ski lodge on a snowmobile and found me."

She didn't go any further into the story for now. She knew, uneasily, that Tony was going to hear about the night she spent with Sverenson in the deserted cabin. She wanted to tell him her version before he heard it from the gossips on the crew. But she nervously shied away from the delicate matter for now.

Tony listened with an expression of deep concern. "We never should have let you come up here alone. Mike could have waited until I finished that assignment back home so we could have left together."

Katy thrust her arm through Tony's as they started slowly toward the lodge. "Well, you know how impatient Mike gets when he's hot for a story. He was so afraid I'd miss something if I waited until Sverenson was embroiled in the actual shooting of the movie."

"What did you mean when you said you didn't know if there was going to be a story?"

Katy kicked at a rock as they walked together. "Oh, Tony, you know how I felt about this assignment before I ever left New York. I dreaded venturing into the wilderness. And I didn't relish interviewing Craig Sverenson. Well, my premonitions were right. I no sooner get up here than I almost freeze to death in a snowstorm. Then I meet Craig Sverenson and all he's done so far is make me mad."

"You said he saved your life. Why should that make you mad?"

"You don't understand," she said sullenly. The truth was, she didn't entirely understand herself. Craig Sverenson had done more than make her angry. He had disturbed her deeply in a way that had her confused and uneasy. On one level she was irritated and on a deeper level that escaped her understanding she was frightened. As Marsha Trident said, Craig was a complex and enigmatic man. More than that, he was a man who could arouse violent feelings in anyone who associated with him. Marsha had said that those who knew him either loved him deeply or hated him violently. It was not something Katy understood very well or was sure she wanted to understand. She only knew that she had felt a growing disquietude ever since coming in personal contact with Craig Sverenson. Some kind of unexplainable instinct for self-preservation urged her to flee from this place.

That made no sense to her reasoning mind and she

had given up trying to unravel her complex emotions. She had to accept that Craig Sverenson frightened her as much as he angered her and she had to let it go at that.

"I still don't understand," Tony persisted. "Do you mean you're going to drop the story and go back to New York?"

"I may," she said darkly.

"Mike would fire you."

"I know. I'm not sure if I care anymore."

Tony shook his head in bewilderment. "I don't understand you at all, Katy—"

That makes two of us, she thought.

"What could be so bad about this? Look at those magnificent mountains. Smell that clean, invigorating air."

"Right now I'd trade it for good old New York smog and a crowded subway!"

That much she did understand. She was not the outdoors type. True, she'd been awed and impressed when she first saw the Rocky Mountains. But the terrifying experience in the snowstorm had put her back in her proper perspective—a born and bred city girl who found herself in a hostile environment.

They paused at the entrance to the ski lodge. Tony looked puzzled and crestfallen. "I guess if you go back, Mike would send another writer or editor. I'd still go along to do the photo work. But it sure wouldn't be much fun. I was counting on seeing a lot of you on this trip, Katy. I thought it would be more of a vacation than a job."

Katy felt a twinge of guilt at Tony's look of disappointment. Perhaps she was being selfish. Quitting at this point would put Mike and the magazine in a terrific bind. Tony would be unhappy. Her Dad would be disappointed if she gave up so easily. It was true she had been entirely engrossed in her own feelings. That was what Craig Sverenson had done to her, she thought angrily.

She squeezed Tony's hand. "Well, I don't know, Tony. Perhaps I haven't entirely got over nearly losing my life in that snowstorm. It was a terrifying experience. I suppose it left me kind of demoralized. But I won't do anything hasty, I promise. At least I'll stick around to see them shoot the opening scenes. The snow has melted enough for the crew to get up to a spot near the summit of Stony Pass. That's where the headwaters of the Rio Grande begin. I understand we're all going up there toward the end of the week if the weather holds."

Tony's eyes sparkled. "That sounds fabulous! I bet you're going to feel better about this whole project once the expedition really gets underway."

"Don't count on it, Tony. I keep telling you I have negative vibes about this whole darn project and they keep getting stronger."

"Have you had a chance to interview Sverenson yet?"

She thought about the night she spent in the cabin with the movie star and hoped Tony wouldn't notice how red her face got. "Not—not since that first night. He's pretty elusive, keeps dashing off with various big shots who are producing the film. I guess he has a lot of responsibilities," she admitted.

Then she said, "But I have gotten some information about him, second-hand from a gal who does his make-up. She's been on several of his film crews. Seems to know him quite well. Marsha Trident. Right now we're roommates. She's an English girl, very nice. Incidentally, you're going to think you're walking into the General Assembly of the United Nations when you meet the crew. He has a couple of French cameramen, a German lighting expert, some Scandinavians—I'm not sure if they're Norwegians or Swedes. They all talk English but with thick accents. Most of the actors and bit players are Americans, although one Italian has a fairly major role, I understand. I swear there's an Arab skulking around in the shadows and I haven't figured out what *he* does."

"Maybe he's the producer with the money," Tony grinned.

"That figures," she admitted. "Oh, Marsha dropped a small bombshell on me the day I arrived. Guess whom they've picked to play the lead female role?"

"I wouldn't have the faintest idea."

"Dolores Ramon."

"The Mexican sexpot?"

"Yes. You know she's Craig's ex-wife?"

Somehow the words brought an unpleasant feeling bubbling up inside her.

Tony whistled. "Sure. *Personality Magazine* did an article on her a few years back. I remember reading it. I think it was about the time she dr..... d Craig Sverenson for that producer. Say, she's one gorgeous woman."

Katy shrugged, "That's a matter of opinion. Anyway, she's joining the expedition when it works down the river to Albuquerque."

"That should liven things up. Dolores Ramon and Craig Sverenson back together again, filming steaming love scenes. Katy, you have to stick around for this!" Tony cried. "It's dynamite."

"Dynamite," she said, slowly, "is a dangerous substance that can blow people into little bitty pieces. . . ."

The spring weather held, growing even warmer and that weekend the camera crews loaded their equipment into four-wheel drive vehicles and prepared to move up to the headwaters of the Rio Grande to film the opening scenes of the movie.

Katy and Tony were standing beside the truck in which they would be given rides, when a shadow fell over them.

Katy looked up to see Craig Sverenson astride a huge black horse. Silhouetted against the sun, the big actor looked gigantic and threatening. "Well, if it isn't our little city tenderfoot," he chuckled. "Sure you're brave enough to make this trip? It's not exactly going to be like riding a carriage through Central Park."

Katy glared at him. If she'd had any qualms about the trip to the higher elevation, he had just made her angry enough to forget them. "I certainly do intend to make the trip," she said coldly. "Unless you have any objections."

He leaned on his saddle horn with a creaking of leather, giving her an insolent smile. "No objections whatsoever. Just try not to get lost this time."

Then he straightened and rode away. Katy stood there, fuming. "Do you see what I mean?" she exploded. "The man is insufferable."

Tony gave her a slightly amused look, shrugged, then clambered into the truck. Several 35mm cameras were slung around his neck.

Katy continued to stare at Sverenson who had ridden to one of the vehicles, which was loaded with filming equipment, and was giving the driver instructions. Her eyes were bright with anger. "Tenderfoot, indeed!" she muttered. "I'll show him."

After the next few hours of bouncing over rugged

terrain and nonexistent roads, often at forty-five degree angles, Katy decided that it was not her feet that were getting tender.

They had climbed to an alpine-like region over 12,000 feet high. She found herself breathing faster as the air grew thinner. But she experienced a feeling of exhilaration in the high, dry, cool air. They were in the high backbone of the Rockies in a region of breathtaking splendor. They rode through thick green grasses. The meadows and slopes were painted every color of the rainbow by acres of alpine flowers. Once she caught sight of an elk bounding through the grass. Tony told her they might also see mountain sheep, deer or bear in this area.

At last they came to a small brook of clear icy water formed from melting snowbanks and mountain springs. This modest creek was the beginning of "The Big River"—the Rio Grande.

Here the party set up a camp since they would be filming in the area for several days. Tents were pitched. The heavy equipment was unpacked. Katy found she would be sharing a tent with Marsha Trident and two other women.

Tony was busy with his cameras, getting candid shots of the actors and film crew as they went about their business of preparing to shoot the first scenes of the movie. Katy watched the bustle of activity for a while, then wandered off by herself, entranced by the beauty of the rippling stream. She sat on a boulder, listening to the melody of the crystal clear water playing over a rocky bed.

Her solitude was interrupted by a masculine voice. "I see you are still with us."

Startled, she jerked around to see Craig Sverenson standing over her. He was dressed in scuffed leather boots and faded blue jeans. His checkered flannel shirt was open at the throat, revealing the curling hairs of his broad chest. A western hat was pushed back from his high forehead. His sea-green eyes, flecked with brown, so much the colors of this rugged countryside, were regarding her in a disconcerting manner.

"What do you mean?" she asked coolly.

He clambered down, his boots thudding into the ground and creating a small avalanche of pebbles from the weight of his giant frame. He sat beside her. She felt disturbed and uneasy by the impact of his presence that seemed to send out shock waves. Nervously she inched away from sitting too close to him.

"Well," he observed, "that was a pretty rough trip up here for a city girl."

Her eyes narrowed. "I'm not all that fragile."

His disturbing gaze roamed down her figure and back to her flushed face. Why did her heart have to pound so when he looked at her that way?

"I know," he murmured, with an inflection that reminded her of that night in the cabin with him. "You're not fragile. Delicate, perhaps, like a lovely hothouse flower not accustomed to the rigors of outdoor life—the wind and sun and harshness of the seasons."

Katy said furiously, "You're never going to let me forget how you had to pick me out of that snowbank, are you? Okay, so I got lost that night and nearly froze. That doesn't mean I'm fragile or delicate. I'm a perfectly healthy, strong normal woman. I just happen to prefer civilization to sunburn and mosquito bites." Then she said, "Aren't you supposed to be back there with your film crew?" And she looked away, angry that he could upset her so easily.

But he settled back, resting his broad shoulders

against the boulder as if he expected to stay for a while. "We're not going to do any actual shooting until in the morning. I thought it would be a good time to have a chat with you."

"Why?" she asked, her voice as chilly as the water scrambling over the rocks below them.

"Correct me if I'm wrong," he said slowly, "but I was under the impression that you were here to interview me for a magazine article. So far I haven't been interviewed."

"So far," she retorted, "I haven't been able to get within thirty feet of you."

"I apologize. I haven't been a very good host. The details of this business have kept me in a spin the past week. I admit it and I'm sorry. But now I do have a breathing spell. That is, if you still want to talk to me. I seem to recall that night in the cabin that you were threatening to go back home. But then I see you're still with us so can I assume you've changed your mind?"

"Don't assume anything," she replied. "I haven't made up my mind yet whether I'm going to commit myself to doing this story or not. I promised our photographer, Tony Wilkins, that I'd at least stick around while you shot your opening scenes."

Craig tossed a pebble into the stream below them. It added a tiny "splash" to the tinkling sound of the water. Katy could hear the voices of the movie company far above and behind them, just a distant sound. Somewhere a bird was singing. The murmur of the brook was soothing, hypnotic. She felt somehow detached from reality in this isolated sylvan setting. She wondered if the thin atmosphere at this altitude could be responsible for the feeling of being in a dream.

The big actor said, "Perhaps you'd like for me to tell you a bit about the story we're filming?"

She looked back at him. "All right."

"The main character is an outdoor man who yearns for the independence and freedom of the land as it was in the last century, but he finds himself increasingly frustrated and hemmed in by an encroaching, complex, twentieth-century plastic world. He's tried to survive in an urban society, works at various jobs—everything from construction laborer to parking lot attendant. Never can hold a job for long. Gets in fights or trouble with the law, mainly because of his frustration at the pressures that hem him in. Gets in barroom brawls on Saturday night to let off steam. Finally, after some trouble with the law, he hides out, steals a horse and rides up here to the high country. He decides to follow the Rio Grande all the way down through New Mexico and Texas to its mouth at the Gulf of Mexico in search of the freedom that is vanishing. Of course, on the way, he has a romantic encounter with a woman. The title of the film will be *The Last Adventure*."

Katy had listened with growing fascination, temporarily forgetting her own tangled emotions that had become wrought up again at his presence. She was gazing directly at him, seeing beyond his words, getting a sudden insight into this complex enigmatic man who was talking to her. She said slowly, "Your main character . . . he's a man born out of his time and place. A seventeenth-century man who through some trick of fate became displaced into the twentieth century."

"Yes, perhaps—"

She continued to stare at him. "Perhaps the man is Craig Sverenson?"

Their eyes had met in some kind of testing, searching exploration, on a dangerous journey into private depths hidden behind protective barricades. Katy felt an icy

65

chill clutch at her stomach, yet she could not tear her gaze away. Something warned her not to take this journey, that she might be putting herself in a jeopardy she would regret. Equally dangerous was the probing of Craig's gaze into her innermost being. He had seen her half-frozen body naked that night in the cabin, but now she felt with a shudder that he was seeing her much more exposed.

"Perhaps," he said softly," the man *is* Craig Sverenson. What do you think, Katy O'Hara?"

"I—I don't know—" she stammered. Her emotions were caught up in a shattering vortex. She felt both hot and cold. She looked away from him at last, breathing hard.

"You are a perceptive young woman," Sverenson went on in the same very soft voice, as if sharing a confidence. "I can see why you would make a good reporter. Now that you believe you have heard my story, perhaps you could tell the story of Katy O'Hara?"

"I—I have no story," she mumbled. "There is no story about Katy O'Hara."

"Pardon me, but that can't be true. Katy O'Hara is a person. A very special individual who must have thoughts and dreams. . . ."

"Everyone has dreams," she said in a muffled voice.

"And Katy O'Hara's dreams?"

"I—I don't know."

"Are they dreams about a great love? A love Katy O'Hara has known—or knows now?"

"There—there is no great love," she said thickly.

"I find that hard to believe. A young woman as lovely as you, with fire in her eyes and in her heart. Surely there must be someone."

"No . . . well, yes." She thought about Tony and felt

disloyal to him. But Tony, a great love? She had thought about being in love with Tony at times, had even told herself it was love. Yet her feeling for Tony did not fit into this wild and desolate setting, talking to this man who frightened and disturbed her so.

"I—I don't know," she finally said.

"If you are in love, there is no question . . . you *know,*" he said in a quiet, sad voice.

She saw the sadness in his eyes. She suddenly thought about Dolores Ramon, the great love in his life. Was her memory the reason for the sudden look of sadness in those strange green-brown eyes of his?

She felt a stab of unreasoning jealousy at a woman who could evoke such a powerful feeling in a man so strong—and immediately told herself she was insane to be having such feelings. But then this was one of those moments of insanity that come rarely in a lifetime, wasn't it? Wasn't she sharing some kind of temporary insanity with Craig in this interlude when they both dropped all defenses and stood with their souls utterly naked before each other?

What had brought on this madness? Surely they would both regret it later. They would be self-conscious and ill at ease with one another. They would not mention it and pretend it had not happened, but they would see it in each others' eyes and be embarrassed.

She wondered how long this spell would last. But it was rudely shattered by a voice yelling, "Craig! Hey, Craig! Oh, there you are. Hey, man, get your tail up here, will you? We've got a problem with the camera angles you want to use—"

For a moment Craig did not answer. His gaze met with Katy's in a final, lingering moment as if reluctant to return to the harsh world of reality.

Then the heavy bones and sinews of his giant frame

went into action to bring him cat-like to his feet. He bent over and his fingers touched Katy's cheeks with the gentleness of a leaf brushing her in a forest. Then he scrambled back up the bank, sending another small shower of pebbles down.

Slowly her hand moved to her cheek where a spot burned with a strange warmth left by his fingers' touch. Katy felt dazed as she tried to make some sense out of what had happened. Craig had infuriated her as usual when he first joined her here in this romantic setting. But then something totally unexpected, something tinged with magic had transpired between them. She went back over their conversation, thinking about the words and realizing it had been something more than words, an undercurrent of sudden revelation followed by an understanding that had unnerved her. The turning point had come when he described the plot of the movie he was filming. It had touched an emotional response in her. The story was so strong, so moving . . . and so attuned to the man in real life, Craig Sverenson. The story had given her a sudden flashing insight into Craig and in that moment he had become a person she could reach out and touch. A person . . . *simpático*, as the Mexicans say. She had forgotten the antagonism that had existed between them since their meeting, at least for this magic moment. He had let his guard down and she had done the same and they had each allowed the other to have a glimpse of a very secluded corner of their private selves.

Now as the sense of magic began to dissipate and her mind became capable of rational thought again, she felt a growing uneasiness. Now she could understand how Craig Sverenson could have such a devastating effect on women. Until today he had been going out of his way to antagonize her for some reason she didn't entirely understand. But it had given her a healthy defensive weapon against him. She'd been too mad at him to fall under his charm.

Then, so swiftly it had taken her breath away, that had changed and she'd had a demonstration of how it was possible to fall under the man's spell.

She realized that she'd better keep her head level from now on to avoid making an utter fool out of herself. She was going to follow a safe course of either staying out of his way completely or returning to the cool aloofness that had marked her relationship with him until this afternoon.

That night she slept in the warm snugness of a heavy sleeping bag in the tent with her four companions. She dreamed fitfully of a tall, broad-shouldered man astride a giant black horse. He came galloping out of the darkness, snatched her up and carried her across the mountain tops. She awoke, her heart pounding and wondered if she had cried out in her sleep. If she had, her cry had not awakened her companions. She could hear the steady breathing of Martha and the other two women. Katy burrowed more deeply into the warm nest of the sleeping bag and was soon asleep again.

She was awakened at dawn by alarms going off in the camp's tents. Shivering, she dressed in a dark blue ski sweater, warm jeans and boots. The aroma of hot coffee and frying bacon wafted into the tent. She joined the rest of the crew outside who were having breakfast prepared by chuck wagon cooks who had been hired to keep the camera crew and actors well fed.

They had arrived in this alpine area yesterday afternoon when the sun was high and warm. But during the night the high altitude chill had dropped the mercury.

Katy thought the temperature must be near the freezing mark in these early dawn hours. The first rays of sunlight were streaking across the mountain tops, seeking out patches of lingering snow and making them glisten as if they had been sprinkled with diamonds.

"You people believe in getting an early start," Katy muttered, warming her hands on a mug of steaming coffee.

Marsha Trident nodded. "We have a long shooting day ahead of us. Craig wants to get these scenes out of the way as quickly as possible so we can move down to lower ground. He doesn't want to be delayed by another late spring snowstorm."

"He told me something about the story plot yesterday," Katy said slowly.

"What do you think of it?"

"It—it sounds as if it could make a strong movie—" Katy said, self-consciously remembering the emotions she'd experienced when Craig related the plot of *The Last Adventure* to her.

"Yes, I think it will be good. It's terribly important for Craig to make a success of this one, it being his first American-made movie and all . . . as well as his being the director, too."

"He—he seems to fit the part of the story's main character—"

"So you noticed that," Marsha said, giving Katy a quizzical smile.

Katy felt her cheeks grow warm. She concentrated on the mug of coffee she was holding, hiding the confusion she felt.

"Well, it's true," Marsha went on. "I think the character in the story is a mirror of Craig himself—an adventurer born in the wrong century. He just laughs it off when I mention it, but I really think that's why he chose this particular story." Marsha hesitated, then asked casually, "Have you decided to stay with us and write your article, then?"

"I haven't entirely made up my mind," Katy hedged, although she was now leaning strongly in that direction.

"Well, perhaps you'll become involved when we actually get down to shooting. I've been around this business a number of years, but I still find it fascinating. There's an excitement in the air that infects everyone when the production gets underway. You might get hooked," she warned.

Katy said, "I thought the way he described the story, it begins with the main character going from job to job in an urban setting. But you're starting up here in the mountains."

"They don't shoot a story in proper sequence," Marsha explained. "We'll pick up the urban scenes later when we move down from the mountains. It's all a kind of hodgepodge affair until they put it together in the cutting room."

As the sun began to warm and brighten their surroundings, the camera crew became busy with their equipment.

It was Katy's first experience of watching firsthand the actual filming of a motion picture on location. Whatever her negative feelings had been about coming on this journey, she had to admit that being so close to the behind-the-scenes creating of a major motion picture was exciting. Marsha had spoken the truth when she warned it would be easy to become hooked on the tension that gripped the company as the filming began.

They spent two days at the alpine location. Most of the "takes" were of Craig riding along the course of the stream and making camp. One shot that Katy thought was beautiful and effective was taken at night as Craig sat beside his campfire, brewing a pot of coffee. The firelight flickering over his rugged features painted a portrait that was rugged, almost sardonic. He projected with stunning impact his characterization of a hunted, tormented man.

Was he, Katy wondered, merely revealing to the camera a portion of his being that he normally kept hidden from the world?

When the scenes at the Rio Grande headwaters were completed the party moved down into the timberline, following the course of the river through dense forests of spruce, fir and aspen. Craig's beard had been shaved off. The first time Katy saw him clean-shaven, she felt a jolt. She had seen innumerable pictures of him and had seen him on the screen, but he was even more striking in person. His jaw was rugged. His wide mouth seemed capable of being both sensuous and cruel. She caught herself staring at him and, blushing, forced her gaze away.

That night when the camp was set up, she found herself deliberately avoiding Tony Wilkins. She knew he wanted her decision as to whether she was going to stay and do the article or return to New York. It was a decision she had almost made. Despite the discomfort of outdoor life, she wanted to stay. But she wasn't quite ready to give Tony the final word. She sensed he was eager to make the most of the romantic setting while she was here and she wanted to avoid that too. She had been unsettled and confused ever since that idiotic moment she'd spent with Craig beside the stream.

Both to avoid Tony and to do some private thinking she wandered a few hundred feet from the main camp to a spot on a ledge overlooking a deep valley below.

The full moon was spectacular, glittering through the trees, turning patches of snow into silvery pools.

She had been there a few minutes when she heard a rustle behind her and she turned, thinking Tony or Marsha had followed her from camp. Then a scream rose to her lips and stuck there.

Lumbering toward her, clearly defined in patches of moonlight, was a giant grizzly bear.

Katy's body turned into a frozen lump of terror. The huge bear paused and sniffed the air, looking directly at her. She heard a muffled whimper escape her lips. She stared wide-eyed at the beast as if hypnotized.

Then out of the corner of her eyes she saw another movement. A big man was moving slowly and quietly as a cat stalking its prey, seeming to melt from shadow to shadow until he was a few feet from her. "Be very still," Craig Sverenson murmured softly. "Don't make any sudden move. He's not going to hurt you. He's just foraging for food."

Katy wasn't sure that she *could* move. She was petrified with fear, which probably saved her life. Otherwise she would have run screaming in a blind panic.

The three of them, Katy, Craig and the bear remained in the frozen tableau for a minute that dragged on for an eternity. The bear continued to sniff the air, making a low, rumbling sound. Then the great animal suddenly swung around and lumbered away.

Katy felt her legs turn to water. Her senses reeled. The trees revolved around her.

Strong arms caught her just before she crumpled. "It's all right," Craig said reassuringly. "He's gone. You're safe."

She clung to him, sobbing. A chill wracked her body as reaction seized her. She was grateful for the strength of his powerful arms. She hid in them, pressing her face against his broad chest. She stayed there for several minutes, drawing strength from him.

Finally she got ahold of herself. She stepped away from him, wiping her tears with the back of her hand. She swallowed hard. Her eyes suddenly blazed and she raised her chin. "Well, aren't you going to make a sarcastic remark about me being a cowardly tenderfoot? You haven't missed an opportunity so far to remind me how inept I am in the wilderness. I guess I just proved it again."

He was gazing at her soberly, his face half hidden by shadows. She expected to hear his derisive chuckle followed by a cutting bit of sarcasm. But he surprised her by saying, "That could have happened to anyone. And I don't blame you for being frightened. Strong men can turn into jelly facing a bear that size. I don't think you were in any real danger. Wild animals unusally don't attack unless they are provoked. Although, of course, you never can be sure what an animal might do."

She was too surprised to reply. She had been braced for his usual ruthless sarcasm. His tone of sympathy and understanding unnerved her all over again and fresh tears trickled down her cheeks. Finally she stammered, "That's the second time you've risked your life to come to my rescue. I'm trying to think how to thank you."

He moved closer to her, his steady gaze probing deeply. She could not read his face. This time he kept his inner self hidden from her. But a fire kindled in his eyes that made her knees tremble again. She felt as helplessly immobilized as when she'd faced the bear. Again his strong arms were around her but this time in a demanding rather than protecting manner. For a

74

moment she could only look at him helplessly. Then his lips were burning on hers, softly, experimentally at first, tasting their quivering essence, then growing hungry and fierce.

Her response was shattering, bursting like a sky rocket from some dark, primitive corner that she had never dreamed existed in her. The sky rocked, flared to dizzying heights and exploded in a myriad of stars behind her closed eyes. She had lost all control of her lips that were returning his kiss as savagely as he had given his, her arms that were clinging to him desperately and her body pressing eagerly the hard contours of his muscular body. She heard a distant moan and realized it came from her own throat.

At last the kiss ended. She tried to force her rubbery legs to move. She got her senses back and was aghast at the loss of control over her primitive desires. Never before in her life had she responded in such an abandoned, wanton manner to a man's kiss. He had caught her in a vulnerable moment, she told herself, when she was in an emotional turmoil over the bear frightening her half to death. It was the only explanation her rational mind could conceive for her response to a man who had angered her so when she first met him—a man all her rational instincts warned her was nothing but a heartless, egotistic predator who treated women as callously as a game hunter regarded his trophies.

"You asked how you could thank me—" he reminded her, a self-confident smile on his lips.

She despised him for that look of triumph. She despised herself with equal ardor for being the willing victim for tonight's conquest. "I certainly did not mean it that way," she said, her voice brittle with ice.

"Nevertheless," he went on in a mocking tone that further infuriated her, "you obviously enjoyed it as much as I did. And would again," he added with cutting insinuation.

"No—certainly not again!" she flung back at him. "You happened to catch me in a weak moment. You took advantage of my frightened state over the bear. Don't get the wrong idea about me, Craig Sverenson."

"I don't think I've got the wrong idea, Katy. Quite the contrary, I think I have your number. You are an attractive, self-assured young woman who until tonight has never fully been aroused. You may hate me as your tone indicates you do, but you also know I hold the key to your passion."

"I do hate you!" she stormed.

He shrugged. "Perhaps. But later tonight, you'll spend some time thinking about our kiss and you'll find yourself with a hunger you didn't know existed before. I know because I feel that hunger for you. I find you a disturbingly attractive young woman, Katy O'Hara, a woman I long to possess—and will before this journey ends."

"Never!" she gasped. "I know all about you, Craig Sverenson. And I don't intend to become another conquest, a passing diversion to keep you from remembering how much you long for Dolores Ramon!"

His face went white. She felt a moment of triumph, knowing she had struck a vital spot. But then the cold anger in his eyes replaced her triumph with a stab of fright.

Nevertheless she held her ground. "You're right," she admitted. "I did respond to your kiss, more shamelessly than I care to remember. But you can be sure it will never happen again."

She started to walk away but a powerful hand caught her wrist, whirled her back to him. The anger she had aroused by her impulsive remark about his ex-wife burned in his eyes with cold fury. This time his embrace was harsh, his lips cruel. He kissed her with savage fury and she tried to fight free of him, but he did not allow her to escape. He held her in his powerful embrace until her muscles went limp and the unwanted fire sprang again into an inferno within her. As if to further demean her, he thrust his hand under her ski sweater, exploring her tender flesh, searching out her quivering bosom.

Finally, as if he had cruelly proved his point, he released her and stalked off into the night.

She stood there, disheveled, her lips bruised, her heart pounding painfully, and she thought she would have been safer with the bear.

Chapter Five

"So you got hooked just as I predicted," Marsha grinned.

Sverenson and his entourage were back at the ski lodge, having completed filming the scenes in the higher altitudes where the Rio Grande was born of melting snow and mountain springs. Now preparations were underway to move down to the desert regions of New Mexico where more location scenes would be filmed. Katy and Marsha were in their room, repacking for the next leg of the journey.

Katy had just informed Marsha that she'd made the decision to continue on with the film company and write the article as originally planned. Marsha's statement about her getting "hooked" had flustered her and brought a scorching blush to her cheeks. Was Marsha hinting that she knew about Craig's kissing her? Filming crews were notorious gossips, Katy knew, and she felt both angry and humiliated that her privacy had been invaded. "I—I don't know what you mean—" she said sharply.

"Don't you remember?" Marsha reminded her mildly. "I warned you that there's an infectious excitement when a film production gets underway and you might get hooked."

"Oh . . . that," Katy said, relieved. "Yes, I remember."

Marsha continued to regard her in an amused, speculative manner. "I was wondering what made you change your mind. By the way, I haven't heard you mention lately how much you detest Craig Sverenson. Has the man's charm done you in too, love?"

The hot spots returned to Katy's cheeks. "Certainly not! I feel exactly the same about him. He's an infuriating egotist. However, I will admit that I'm impressed by the story he's filming and the powerful meaning he's putting into his role. The man is a consummate actor. I'll certainly grant him that."

The direction the conversation had taken was disturbing to Katy. She wished Marsha would let up on her. At the moment she wasn't sure herself why she had made her decision to remain and do the article. She had been in a state of confusion since the night she had been frightened by the bear and then emotionally devastated by Craig's kisses.

During rational moments when she was capable of sane thoughts, she berated herself for the traitorous side of her character that had melted so shamelessly in the fire of Craig's kisses. She had thought her moral fiber to be stronger than that. It was demoralizing to discover that a man's caress could so utterly wreck her emotional equilibrium. In those saner moments she thought she did despise him—and despised him all the more for his infuriatingly correct prediction that she would think about the kisses and feel a hunger she had not experienced before. It was true! When her thoughts strayed in that direction, she felt a warmth and sweet yearning possess her until she could think of nothing else.

Was that why she had decided to stay on? It was a dangerous decision, courting disaster. She tried to convince herself that she had made the decision because she had become fascinated with the story, the acting and the filming process. But a small voice of honesty nagged her that she could no more tear herself away from Craig Sverenson at this point than a sky diver could resist the hypnotic lure of dangerous excitement just before stepping off into space.

As if reading her thoughts, Marsha persisted, "I wouldn't be too certain of yourself where Craig is concerned. Not many women are immune to that man's charm. You may start out disliking him, as you say you do, and find yourself having entirely different feelings before we're through making this movie."

"Just what are you getting at?" Katy demanded testily.

Marsha shrugged. "Oh, nothing, I suppose. I'm just an incurable romantic. I've noticed the way you look at him sometimes. And incidentally, the way *he* sometimes looks at *you*, which is rather surprising. Craig doesn't usually pay any attention to any special woman when he's engrossed in doing a film."

Katy felt herself growing flustered again. "I—I wasn't aware I was looking at him in any 'special' way. He is the subject of an in-depth article I'm writing, after all. I have to study the man, his various moods and traits. I certainly didn't notice him looking at me in the way you imply. Actually, I thought I was something of an annoyance to him."

Marsha smiled. "Oh, well, I'm probably seeing something that isn't there. I told you I was a romantic."

"Yes, I have no personal interest in Craig Sverenson," Katy said, trying not to listen to a small voice within her that shouted *liar!* "Anyway, I have a beau. Tony Wilkins. I've been seeing Tony for some time and I think he's getting serious."

Why did she say *"he's* getting serious" instead of *"we're* getting serious"?

"Tony's nice," Marsha nodded. "He's made a lot of friends with the crew. Seems to be a very fine photographer, too. I'd say you have a winner in Tony. Certainly a lot safer than getting involved with Craig. Tony impresses me as the nice solid type a woman can depend on. I'd say that embarking on a romantic venture with Craig Sverenson would be like setting out on a stormy sea in a leaky old tub."

"Sounds as if you're trying to warn me about something," Katy said slowly, giving Marsha a searching look.

"Well, perhaps I am. I suppose I know Craig quite well, having worked on his film crews so often. Or maybe what I really mean is that I don't know him very well at all and neither does anyone else. And that's what's dangerous about him. The part about Craig that may be volatile is how much he's still involved with his ex-wife and with her doing this picture with him. . . ." Marsha shrugged. "You could be letting yourself in for some grief if you did start having some romantic notions about Craig. Now tell me it's none of my business and we'll finish packing."

"Okay," Katy grinned. "It's none of your business."

Katy and Tony returned their rented cars to the agency in Alamosa and from that point on traveled with the filming company in their vehicles. They drove out of the coolness of the mountains and high plains of Colorado to the sunbaked deserts of New Mexico, following the course of the Rio Grande.

Now they were entering the land of the Pueblo Indians, where Francisco Vazquez de Coronado and his Spanish Conquistadores had searched in vain for the seven cities of gold.

It was at one of the Pueblo ruins that Sverenson's party made their next major stop. The area was now a national park. Katy learned that Sverenson had made arrangements with the Department of the Interior to film scenes for his movie among the ruins of the ancient Indian village.

They arrived late in the afternoon when the slanting rays of the sun turned the crumbling red clay walls into fiery hues.

Entranced by the silent mood of desolation that now hung over the deserted ruins, Katy left the motor homes and trucks of the film company in the parking area and wandered among the remains of structures in the ancient city. The pueblo was located on a hill commanding a view of the rolling countryside for miles in every direction. Below them, to the west, was the great river, the Rio Grande, that had sustained the lives of the Pueblo cities in this arid land.

Katy thought of the men, women and children, who had lived their daily lives here hundreds of years ago.

She wondered if their ghosts lingered in the shadows of the silent walls. A shiver touched her body.

"One can see why they thought the cities were built of gold," a voice said behind her.

Startled, Katy turned. The tall figure of Craig Sverenson loomed as if part of the ghostly shadows.

"What?" she asked, aware that her heart was beating at a faster rate now, partly because he had startled her but partly because of his overpowering presence.

"The Spanish explorers, the *Conquistadores*—the "conquerers," he explained. "They thought some of these pueblos were built of gold."

"Yes, I know." What school child hadn't read about the mythical seven cities of gold?

"I was pointing out how the legend could have started." He made a sweeping gesture toward the parts of the city bathed in the dying rays of the setting sun. "The color of the clay looks almost golden in the sunset."

"Yes," she nodded, acutely aware of her seclusion with this powerful, disturbing man here among the ghostly shadows and silent walls of a dead village.

"Poor Coronado," Craig said, his brown-flecked green eyes gazing across the crumbling red clay, across the river and into another century. "He started out from Mexico City with his banners waving bravely, his soldiers on horseback, his heart filled with the magnificent dream of conquering cities of gold. His dream turned to red clay here in the desert."

Again Katy felt the peculiar shiver. Craig seemed to be gazing on a ghostly scene being replayed before his eyes across the fading sky of twilight. "I—I have the strange feeling that you're remembering it . . . as if you were there. . . . she stammered.

His gaze moved toward her. He had become a part of the shadows now. Was he really a man of another century, a visitor to her time and place, brought here by some unexplainable time warp?

His chuckle was soft. "You seem to imply I was one of Coronado's soldiers in another life?"

"Perhaps," she murmured, not really sure of what she meant. "It is easy to visualize you in the breastplate armor and plumed melon-shaped helmet of a Conquistador, astride a giant horse . . . strong . . . ruthless . . . cruel—" Her voice faded.

Again his gaze moved toward the sky, painted scarlet and purple now by a last wild splash of color from the sun's palette. "I think it would have been a good time to have lived," he nodded slowly. "In a raw land, where a man's limitations were only the horizon and the measure of his own strength. Perhaps I would have liked to have been one of Coronado's men. Or I might have been even happier as one of the Indians his men fought, who were even more a part of the land."

There was a sudden flare of light as he struck a match to light the pipe clenched in his strong, white teeth. The brief, ruddy glow of the match lighted the craggy lines of his face, the bronzed face of an outdoorsman whipped by the wind and burned by the sun, the strong jaw and broad mouth, the lines of crow's feet etched into the corner of eyes familiar with blue skies and distant horizons.

Katy felt her heart lurch, felt that bitter-sweet yearning. What was happening to her, she wondered with a feeling of panic. He was a devastating package of rugged manhood. She tried to remember how she had once despised him, but that feeling was elusive now. In its place was a mingling of fright and fascination.

What kind of man was he? The more she was around

him, the less she knew him. But the more fascinating he became.

Now he moved to her side, slipped his arm through hers and slowly led her along the paths of the village as he talked. The masculine scent of his aromatic pipe tobacco, mingled with shaving lotion and leather, surrounded him. She was acutely aware of the touch of her arm in his, the warmth of his body moving close to hers. She was mesmerized by the timber of his baritone voice, talking softly in the twilight.

"You know, it was the discovery of maize—Indian corn—that revolutionized the life of the Indians of this region," he said. He puffed thoughtfully on his pipe, absorbed in a subject that obviously held a great interest for him. "The entire Indian community life of these tribes along the Rio Grande revolved around the planting and cultivation of their crops—especially corn. The most valuable sacred offering they could make to their gods was crushed corn."

"So," Katy said, "they built these cities out of river clay near their fields."

"Yes, but not at first. The ancestors of the Pueblo Indians were the cliff dwellers. They built entire cities in the cliffs and stored their grain in the dry caves of the rocky cliffs. Those scattered cliff cities are located in southwestern Colorado, northeastern Arizona and northern New Mexico."

As he talked, she realized she was being introduced to yet another facet of this complex man. She had seen Craig Sverenson, the rugged outdoorsman, the actor, the matinee idol, the charmer. Now she realized he was also a man of sensitivity and intelligence, well-informed, well-read.

As they wandered in a relaxed fashion through the ruins of the village, Katy became aware of a subtle new dimension of their relationship. In the mood of this moment, she neither despised him nor feared him as an emotional threat. He seemed content simply to enjoy her companionship, as if he had been lonely and was pleased to have a friend with him to share the mood created by the silent and desolate ruins of a city from another age. Perhaps, she thought uneasily, in this mood he was an even greater threat. For she found herself absorbed in his conversation, deeply interested in what he was telling her of Indian history and filled with a growing admiration for his intellect. She began to wonder if she could ever know all there was to know about him.

He was saying, "For some reason that is a mystery—since the Indians had no written language to record it—toward the end of the thirteenth century, the cliff dwellers abandoned their mountain homes and migrated down to the valley of the big river that they called the P'osoge . . . the river we know as the Rio Grande. Here they built their adobe pueblos. At the time of the Conquistadores there were eighty of these Indian cities. Today there are only nineteen Pueblo villages left."

He hesitated. "But I must be boring you with all this. I didn't mean to deliver a lecture."

"You're not boring me at all," she said quickly. "I find it fascinating. You must have done a lot of study on this subject to know so much about it."

He shrugged. "I'm far from an authority. I must do considerable research on the background for my film settings, though. And I do enjoy reading about history and archaeology."

"You're full of surprises," she murmured.

"Why?"

"It's a contradiction. You have such a macho image—so much the rugged outdoorsman, the adventurer, daredevil. I don't think your public envisions you with a book in your hand."

He merely chuckled. Then he said, "Well, I like to talk and now I have an audience—a most attractive and lovely audience. Would you like to know something about the community life of these Pueblo Indians? Perhaps you can use it in your article."

Her cheeks warmed at his momentary lapse onto more personal territory. But she kept her reply friendly, yet guarded. "Indeed I would. I was trying to imagine what this city must have been like when it was alive with people . . . children playing, men and women going about their daily routines. . . ."

"Very well, but promise to stop me if I start to bore you or sound too pedantic."

He fussed with his pipe for a moment, then continued, "Well, they lived very much a communal life. The land, the religious buildings and religious ceremonial objects, even the pueblo itself, were all owned by everybody jointly in the community. Everybody lived on the same scale. Their rooms were alike. They owned about the same amount of food, clothing and furniture. They all held the same views and ideas about their work and their religion. Even their designs in making things followed the same pattern down to the smallest detail. To be different from anyone else was in bad taste and aroused suspicion and displeasure in the community. Originality was frowned upon. There was no place for individualism."

"Pure communism!" Katy gasped. Then she shook her head. "I don't think I can visualize you as an Indian brave living very comfortably in *that* social order!"

"I guess not," he admitted. "I think I would have

preferred to have been a plains Indian, hunting the buffalo."

"How did these Pueblo Indians learn to make their adobe buildings?"

"Who knows?" he shrugged. "They may have found earlier tribes who had stumbled on the method of mixing river clay with straw and letting it dry in the sun to become as hard as bricks. Probably the Pueblo Indians remembered the architectural designs of their old cliff cities. The walls of their pueblo buildings were built up by scooping handfuls of adobe and plastering and patting it over surfaces. Layer upon layer was added until the walls were thick enough to support ceiling beams. Cross branches were laid on the beams and plastered over to form a ceiling and roof. Once the roof was smooth and strong enough, it served as the floor for a second story and eventually a third story was added. Pretty soon they had a structure like a giant beehive with many cells. There were no ground level doors. They used ladders to go from one level to the next.

"In the village each family was allotted a single small room, about twelve by fourteen feet. The only entrance was through the roof which was reached by the ladders. The walls of the rooms were whitewashed with a mixture of water and gypsum which they found in the river country. Smoke from the family's cooking fire, which was built in the middle of the floor, went up through the doorway in the roof."

They paused before a low mound which had an opening like the entrance to a subterranean chamber.

"That's a *kiva*," he explained. "An underground room where their religious ceremonies took place."

"A temple?"

"Something like that. The religious ceremonies were conducted by priests and men of the village who wore grotesque masks which symbolized certain gods. It was all very secretive. The women and children believed the figures wearing the masks were real gods who had come from the rivers and mountains to visit them. They were frightened and awed at the sight of these gods dancing about.

"The Pueblo people had an effective way of dealing with juvenile delinquency," he chuckled. "Once a year, a member of the tribe would dress up in the most hideous mask he could devise and come howling into the town to scare the youngsters out of their wits. He'd visit the homes of children who had misbehaved and hop around making fierce gestures and tell the kids he was going to take the naughty children of the village off to his cave and eat them. The parents went along with the ritual, pretending to be as frightened as the children and begged the ugly monster not to carry off their children. He'd get tearful promises from the badly frightened youngsters to behave before he'd finally leave. You might say the bogyman was very real to a child living in a Pueblo Indian village.

"Introduction to manhood was a shocking experience for the Pueblo boys. When a boy reached a certain age, the youngster was taken before the 'gods' gathered in the *kiva*. Now put yourself in the boy's place. All his life he had believed these frightening creatures to be supernatural. Suddenly the masks were jerked off. Before him, instead of gods, stood the men of the village, perhaps his own uncle."

"How dreadful!" Katy cried. "Those poor boys. To leave them so suddenly with no more illusions."

"Yes. Well, perhaps it was better to do it all at once

like that and get it over with," he murmured. "In our society, we spend a lifetime exchanging illusions for reality."

There was a note of sadness, a hint of bitterness in his voice. Was he thinking about his tragic marriage to the beautiful Dolores Ramon, Katy wondered with a curious stab of pain.

"Now you—you sound like a cynic. . . . she murmured.

"Just a realist," he replied.

He was silent for a moment as if withdrawing into a private place to be alone with his brooding thoughts. Then he continued their conversation. "But back to the boys in the village. Once the boy was introduced into manhood, he was accepted into the secret societies. His lips were sealed, under threat of great punishment, never to reveal the secret of the masks in the *kiva*. The whole thing has powerful, dramatic possibilities. I want to use it somehow in the film. I think we'll have the hero spend a night in this deserted pueblo during his wanderings. He could fall asleep and see the *kiva* ceremony in a dream sequence."

Katy nodded. "Anyone falling asleep in these spooky ruins could certainly have nightmares about them. I feel almost certain if I looked down that entrance to the *kiva,* I'd see the ghosts of those priests dancing around in their hideous masks. I'll probably dream about them myself," she added with a shiver.

Craig laughed. "You have quite an imagination, little tenderfoot."

"I was hoping you wouldn't call me that anymore," she flared.

He raised an eyebrow. "Does it make you angry?"

"The way you use it is an insult. You sound so darned

superior and patronizing. I've been enjoying this conversation. I thought we were becoming friends."

He gave her a long, searching look, his eyes burning like smoldering coals in the twilight shadows. "Can a man and woman be friends when he's trying to seduce her and she's determined to rebuff him?"

Spots of anger burned her cheeks. She glared at him. "You can be quite crude!"

"Crude? I thought I was being honest . . . have been honest since that night we were snowbound in the cabin. I find you disturbingly attractive, little Irish girl."

"So you're lusting after me."

"That's one way of putting it. Now who's being crude?"

He was regarding her in an amused, mocking way that further angered her.

Before she could reply, he went on, "Furthermore, you feel the same desire. The chemistry between us is boiling. When it's like that between a man and woman, it's hard to fight. It doesn't happen that often. Why do you keep denying it?"

"Because I have some concern for my own feelings, which you apparently overlook!" she retorted. "It's not that simple for a woman to indulge herself in primitive desires. You could have your little fling, satisfy your hunger and go on to your next woman without a look backward! That kind of surrender to me means a deeper commitment. It so happens I have a fine young man who wants to make that kind of commitment and I'm going to save myself for him. I'm not throwing away my self-respect for a moment of insanity. . . ."

He gazed at her silently as the air between them vibrated with electric tension. His face was lost in the deep shadows. It was impossible for her to see his expression.

When he finally spoke, it was in the objective, impersonal tone he had used earlier in describing life in the pueblo villages. "Well, let's see a bit more of the pueblo before we join the others."

He knocked out his pipe, thrust it in a shirt pocket and began walking slowly. She moved beside him but now she did not link her arm in his. She kept a space between them. The evening had taken an upsetting, disconcerting turn. The fact that a giant full moon was rising, threatening to cast a subversive mood of romantic magic over the ruins, did not east her emotional turmoil.

Craig was talking again about village life of the Indians, as casually impersonal as if the brief emotional encounter between them had not taken place.

At last their wandering course took them to the outer walls of the pueblo near the parking area where the camera crew was camped for the night.

He gazed down at her. She felt the steady thudding of her heart. Was he going to kiss her? Her body trembled. She doubted if she'd have the strength to push him away if he took her in his arms.

But he did not. He simply gazed at her as if she were some kind of perplexing riddle he was trying to master. Then, in a gesture he had used once before, he touched her cheek lightly and said, "I've enjoyed our conversation. Good night."

He turned and dissolved into the dark shadows of the ruined village, leaving her with a sense of unreality. Where was he? Had he simply vanished? Had she really been talking with him this past hour or had it been a dream?

She shook her head slowly, baffled by her own

mental and emotional confusion. Finally she walked back to the parking area.

Katy had an evening meal consisting of a TV dinner warmed in the microwave oven in one of the motor homes. Tony Wilkins came by, carrying some of his camera equipment. "I'm planning to take some time exposures of the village in the moonlight. Want to come along?"

"Yes, I would," she said, realizing she needed to be with Tony tonight. She needed to get her feet back on the ground and her head on straight again. She felt sane and normal around Tony. Perhaps her heart didn't beat erratically nor her knees wobble when she was with Tony. But she felt safe and secure. Tony didn't frighten and upset her. The world was a saner place when she was with Tony, and that could be important too.

They found a suitable place in the ruins for Tony to set up his tripod. "This should be beautiful," he murmured.

Katy helped by holding some of the photography equipment while Tony busied himself with his camera.

After the time exposures were completed, they sat on a wall together. The moon was out in full, round splendor now, bathing the crumbling pueblo with platinum highlights and inky shadows.

"Pretty romantic," Tony said, holding her hand.

She squeezed his fingers, enjoying his companionship. The lovely night and Tony's presence had brought a measure of calm back to the battleground that had been raging in her heart. She sensed that Tony wanted to kiss her and that was fine too.

It was a lingering kiss. No sky rockets going off behind her closed eyelids. No frightening, overpowering hungers exploding in primitive shadows of her darker self. Just sweetness. Warmth. Security. Knowing that Tony would never deliberately hurt her. Would not use her to satisfy selfish desires, then walk away leaving her to cope with her own broken heart.

"Katy," Tony said huskily. "I want to talk to you about something important. You and me—"

Katy pressed her fingers gently against his lips. "Not yet—not now, Tony."

"But—"

"Please. Let's—let's not get serious tonight. I—I need to do some more thinking . . . get some things straightened out in my mind. Now kiss me again and then take me back to camp."

They gathered up the camera equipment and started back to the camping area. It was at that point when Katy became aware of a solitary figure seated on one of the ancient walls, outlined darkly against the sky.

Craig Sverenson! How long had he been sitting there, alone, in brooding silence? With an odd feeling of consternation she wondered, had he seen Tony kiss her?

Chapter Six

Katy's portable typewriter clattered with a machine-gun-like staccato. She was so deep in concentration, she wasn't aware that Marsha Trident had entered the motor home until Marsha paused behind her and commented, "You really do burn up the keys on that thing."

Katy stopped typing and frowned at the paper in her machine. "I thought it was about time I started the first rough draft of my article. I've made a bundle of notes and now I'm trying to get them into some coherent form."

Marsha took a canned soft drink from the refrigerator, popped it open and arranged her long-legged form comfortably on a convenient sofa. She glanced around the elegant motor home and muttered, "Color telley, microwave oven, thick carpets, 'fridge. How do you Americans do it? This thing is more luxurious and better equipped than a lot of digs my friends live in back home." She took a sip of her drink and asked, "How's your article coming along?"

Katy stood up, stretched her cramped body and massaged her neck. "Not too well," she complained. "Is there another drink in the refrigerator?"

"Several."

Katy chose one, opened it and relaxed in a seat facing Marsha. "I'm discovering that Craig Sverenson is a baffling man to write about. Just when I think I'm grasping some understanding of the man, he shows me a completely new side to his character that throws my entire concept of him out of focus. I'm beginning to think he has several clones running about, each one identical on the outside but with their own character traits."

"Interesting way of putting it. If you'd been out on the set this morning, you would have seen another Craig Sverenson—one that might have sent chills up your back."

Katy's eyes widened with sudden interest. "What do you mean?"

Marsha sipped her drink thoughtfully. "You remember my saying that at times Craig can be a pussycat? Well, he can also be pretty violent. He demonstrated that this morning. We just had a bit of excitement that has us all shook up. No more shooting for today, I venture to say."

"And I picked this morning to sit in here and type!" Katy wailed. "Tell me what happened."

"It wasn't pretty, love. A man tried to sabotage the film. A has-been actor named Ronald Crowder. He's been hanging around for several days. Craig ran him off day before yesterday. This morning he sneaked back. One of the film crew caught him in the truck where they're carrying the footage we've shot to date. He was in the process of destroying all of it."

"Oh, no!" Katy gasped.

Marsha nodded soberly. "Bloody serious business. It could have meant going back to Colorado and starting the whole thing over at the cost of who knows how much. Probably more than the budget could have absorbed. Craig might have had to scrap the entire movie. Fortunately when they caught Ronald, he'd only succeeded in ruining some of the last few reels. It will mean reshooting on this location a few extra days, which is bad enough. At any rate it took three strong fellows to pull Craig off Ronald. Can't really say I blame Craig—"

"What have they done with the man?" Katy asked.

"Craig called in the local sheriff's department. They hauled Ronnie off to jail. I imagine Craig will file every charge against him known to the legal profession."

Katy was silent for a moment, absorbing this surprising and shocking development. Then she said with a puzzled frown, "You call this man by his first name— Ronald, 'Ronnie.' Were you acquainted with him?"

"Oh, yes. He was pretty well known in movie circles a few years back. Had a number of fairly good secondary roles. Worked in a couple of Craig's films, as a matter of fact. That's when the trouble started."

"What trouble? Why in heaven's name did the man want to sabotage Craig's movie?"

"That's quite a story, love. Might be worth your looking into for your article. Ronald Crowder despises Craig Sverenson. He'd do anything to get back at Craig. I don't think he'd stop at murder, if it came to that."

"But why? What did Craig do to him?"

"According to Ronnie, Craig destroyed his career. Had him thrown off the set of a film Craig was doing and got him blackballed throughout the industry."

"Do you know why Craig did that?"

"Not exactly. I've heard several versions, mostly gossip. It rather depends on whether you're talking with Craig or Ronnie about it. I didn't happen to be working on the particular film where the trouble started between the two of them."

"Hmmm." Katy chewed her lip. Suddenly she was confronted by a situation that puzzled and disturbed her. Was Craig justified in what he had done to the other actor? Or was she about to uncover something distasteful and mean about Craig Sverenson? Had it been some kind of petty professional jealousy that had caused Craig Sverenson to destroy the other man's career? Was Craig after all the villain she had once thought him to be?

The possibility of discovering a black, vicious side to Craig sent a stab of cold pain slicing through her. But she could not ignore this new issue. Not for the sake of her honesty as a writer. And not for her own sake as a woman rapidly becoming emotionally entangled with the man.

"Someone very smart," she began slowly, "once said that if you really want to know the truth about another person, you don't go to his friends—you ask his enemies."

Marsha pursed her lips thoughtfully. "Well, I told you once before that Craig certainly has his enemies. A strong man makes strong friends and strong enemies. I would imagine you'd find Ronald Crowder heading the list of people who hate Craig's guts."

"How can I interview Ronald Crowder?" Katy asked with sudden resolve.

"He's in the local hoosegow," Marsha said. "The gendarmes just hailed him off. I suppose you'd have to see the sheriff in town."

Katy dumped the remainder of her drink in the kitchenette sink and went in search of Tony. She found him talking with some members of the filming crew and called him aside. "Have you heard about the trouble this morning?" she asked.

"Sure. Everybody's talking about it."

"Tony, I want to interview that man."

"The guy who sabotaged the film?"

"Ronald Crowder. I understand they took him off to jail in town. I want you to go with me. We may need some photos of the guy. Apparently there's been some bad blood between this Crowder person and Craig Sverenson for some time. I want to find out what it is. We may be onto something about Craig that isn't very pretty—something he's been keeping under wraps."

"Why don't you ask Craig about it?"

"Oh, I fully intend to. But first I want to hear Crowder's side."

Tony borrowed a truck from a friend he'd made in the film crew. Katy rode beside Tony, her face grim. She felt a dull apprehensive ache. If there was something unpleasant about Craig's past she recoiled from knowing what it was. But her integrity as a reporter demanded that she get at the truth.

The small town sheriff, a florid blustering man whose ancestry—as was so often the case in this area—included a mixture of Indian, Mexican and Anglo, viewed the two big-city Yankee strangers with considerable suspicion. He painstakingly checked their identification, then kept them waiting in an outer office of the small, musty county jail for over an hour. Katy decided that he was weighing his prejudice and suspicion of outsiders against the possibility of bringing the wrath of national news media down on his back. Finally a deputy escorted them back to the cell area of the ancient jail. The place smelled of damp concrete and disinfectant. They faced the prisoner through rusty bars.

Ronald Crowder was a slender man dressed in dark slacks and a rumpled white sport shirt open at the collar. He was nervously chain smoking. Katy saw that his fingers trembled noticeably when he lit a fresh cigarette off the one he'd just smoked down to a stub. She studied his face, curiously seeking a clue to his character. She saw a face that had once been handsome but now was haggard and lined as if ravaged by a lingering illness. There was a purple bruise on his jaw, no doubt the result of his encounter with Craig. His eyes appeared drained. She had the feeling that she was looking at the shell of a man whose inner being had somehow been reduced to ashes. He was probably in his mid-thirties but looked ten years older.

"Mr. Crowder, my name is Katy O'Hara. This is my associate, Tony Wilkins. I'm a writer for *Personality Magazine*. We're doing an article about Craig Sverenson—a kind of in-depth personality profile of Craig combined with a story about this new film he's making."

The prisoner gazed at her with flat, dull eyes. "What do you want from me? You wouldn't want to print what I think of Craig Sverenson."

Katy drew a breath, pushing down the heaviness in her chest. "Perhaps we would," she said slowly. "My editor wants to tell our readers the truth about Craig, whatever it is. We've been traveling with his party since they started filming on location in Colorado. Craig

Sverenson is still something of a mystery to me. I feel I've only scratched the surface in getting to know him. Obviously something happened between the two of you in the past that has made you very bitter toward him. My instinct as a reporter tells me there may be a story there if you want to talk about it."

Crowder puffed on his cigarette, looking at her thoughtfully. "Have you talked with Sverenson about this?"

"Not yet."

"Why not? Seems like the natural thing would be for you to let him tell you about it since you know him."

"That's true. But in a case like this, a reporter likes to dig below the surface. You're the one who's the angry man. You sabotaged Craig's film. Why? You must be carrying a lot of hate around with you. Sverenson might not want me to know all the facts. At least I want to hear from you first. Then I can weigh that against what Craig has to say. I repeat—if you want to talk about it."

Crowder shrugged. "Sure, I'll talk about it. Maybe somebody will print the truth about Craig Sverenson for a change instead of the 'hero' garbage his public relations people hand out. Let me tell you something about Craig—he's a dictator, a ruthless, coldblooded tyrant. If you work in a picture with him, you're okay if you do exactly as he says . . . if you pay homage to his colossal ego. On his sets he's Caesar and you'd better not forget it. You don't try to steal any scenes by being a better actor—and you'd better not become involved with his women. I made both mistakes and he ruined me—took my career and my life away. Craig Sverenson never forgets. You can print that in your magazine!"

Katy stared at the man behind the bars, the dull ache

inside her turning into a cutting pain. His bitterness was a heavy weight in the air. Was he telling the truth? What *was* the truth?

"Can you go more into detail?"

"Sure." Crowder lit a fresh cigarette with shaking fingers. "Five years ago, I had a lot going for me. Ask anybody in the business. Ask my agent—my ex-agent now. I was working all the time. I was going places, getting bigger and bigger parts. Why? Because I was an actor, a damn good actor. Craig Sverenson isn't an actor—he's a personality, like John Wayne or Clark Gable. I was an actor. I was a threat to Craig the minute I walked on the set with him. He sensed it immediately. I knew I was in trouble on that picture. I had a pretty good part and I was going to cut him to ribbons. The reviews were going to say I walked off with the picture. That was my first mistake. Craig wasn't going to take that. The second mistake was a harmless flirtation with Craig's wife. He was married to Dolores Ramon then. If you know anything about the situation, you'd know that Dolores made a play for every new man who came on the set. I was flattered. Dolores is one of the most beautiful women in the world. She'd make any man lose his sense of caution.

"Nothing really all that serious ever happened between us. But Craig was a violently jealous man. He heard rumors about Dolores and me. That was the last straw. Anybody in the industry can tell you the rest of the story. Craig got me thrown out of the picture. He trumped up all kinds of lies about me. I couldn't get work anywhere else. My career went down the tubes. My wife divorced me, taking the kids, the house, the car, the bank account. I'm broke. Down and out. Craig Sverenson did that to me. I can't make any alimony payments and my wife's threatening to have me jailed."

He looked around and a bitter laugh spilled from his lips. "That's a good one on her, isn't it? Craig beat her to it. He said he's going to see that I spend the next five years behind bars. And he'll probably do it. He's a vindictive man. Once he gets it in for somebody, he never lets up."

Ronald Crowder paused, his voice breaking. Tears were trickling down his cheeks. Finally he choked, "That's the real story of Ronald Crowder and Craig Sverenson. Have you got the courage to print it, lady?"

When they were back in the truck, Tony whistled, "That ought to make a nice juicy angle to add to your story. I got some good candid shots of the guy while he was talking, by the way. He was so upset, I don't think he even noticed what I was doing."

Katy's insides were a boiling cauldron of emotions. She was shocked, disillusioned and angry. Mostly angry, she thought. If Ronald Crowder's story checked out to be even partly true, she was going to despise Craig Sverenson to her dying day. How dare he pretend to be a big brave hero type while coldbloodedly destroying another man's life!

Her anger was amplified when she remembered, with a wave of scorching humiliation, how she had responded to Craig's kisses.

"Do you think Crowder's telling the truth?" Tony wondered.

"I sure mean to find out," Katy said grimly. "If what he says is true, I'm going to expose Craig Sverenson to the world for the two-faced rat he is!"

"Crowder's right about one thing: Craig *is* something of a tyrant on the set. I've found out that much, talking to the camera crews and bit players."

Katy nodded. "That's not exactly news. I guess I can forgive him for that. He is a genius when it comes to filmmaking and that kind often are dictatorial. He's a perfectionist. He demands perfection from everyone around him. He does get results. And I certainly don't agree with Ronnie Crowder that Craig is more of a film personality than an actor. He's a darn fine actor. It's the rest of it that makes me sick to my stomach. If Craig ruined that poor man's career just because of professional jealousy and because Crowder was involved with Dolores Ramon—who everyone knows is a tramp—well, Craig's the one who should be thrown into jail!"

When they reached the parking area of the ruins where the movie crew was encamped, Katy shot off in search of Craig. She learned he was in an office that had been set up in one of the big motor homes. She waited, fuming, for a half hour before a secretary permitted her to enter the small office. Craig was seated behind a desk which was piled high with papers.

"Hello, Katy," he said, arising from his office chair. "Sorry to keep you waiting. I've been tied up in a conference. We've had a problem this morning—"

"I know all about it," she said in a tight, cold voice. "That's what I want to talk to you about."

He looked at her with a puzzled expression. "It's just a bit of personal unpleasantness. It couldn't possibly have anything to do with the article you're writing—"

"Oh, but it does! Very much so." Katy had difficulty in keeping her voice level. She felt herself seething with disgust and humiliation. If she was overreacting it was, she knew, because of how she was becoming personally involved with Craig Sverenson. She had started out despising the man. Then seeing him on a daily basis, discovering that she could be so defenseless against his magnetic appeal, learning to admire his talent, his manliness, his sensitivity, she had begun to fall under his spell. Now it was possible he had pulled the wool over her eyes. And she was angry with him and with herself for being so gullible.

In a voice brittle with ice she said, "I've just talked with Ronald Crowder."

Surprise registered in Craig's eyes, followed quickly by an expression of irritation. "I can't imagine why you'd do a thing like that."

"Oh, can't you? You seem to forget that I am a reporter whose assignment is to write a story about the real Craig Sverenson. Now I'm trying to find out just who the real Craig Sverenson is. Is he one of the last heroes of the twentieth century . . . a man bigger than life, brave, daring, resourceful as well as sensitive and intelligent? Or is he a petty, jealousy-ridden sadist who thinks nothing of destroying another man's life?"

A dangerous flush of anger had been spreading over Craig's rugged features. His narrowed eyes glinted fire. "Yes," he said coldly. "I can see that you have been talking with Ronald Crowder—not only talking but listening to him. And apparently believing him."

Craig and Katy faced each other in the tiny room that had grown stifling with steaming anger.

"Well?" Katy demanded. "Are you going to deny the things he said about you?"

Craig's eyes were boiling pits of rage. "Why should I bother? You've apparently accepted what he said. Go ahead and write what you want to. I don't have time to talk about it anymore."

He made a movement as if to show her out.

"Are you telling me that Ronald Crowder told me the truth about what happened between the two of you?"

"I'm not telling you anything!" he threw back at her. "I don't have to explain my life to anybody—especially to a smart aleck little New York tenderfoot who's still damp behind the ears!"

Katy could see she was about to be thrown out of his office. She had no intention of allowing that to happen until she got some answers from Craig Sverenson. With an effort, she got some control of her raging emotions. She swallowed hard, took a deep breath and filtered the rage out of her voice. "Just a minute," she said, planting her feet firmly and placing her hands against Craig's massive chest. "You've not heaving me out of here just yet. Perhaps I did come in here with a chip on my shoulder. Maybe you have a right to be angry. If that's the case I'll apologize in due time. But you must be able to understand my side of this matter. Ronald Crowder has made some dreadful accusations against you. He said—"

"I don't want to hear what that sniveling, poor excuse of a human being has made up to justify his own failures."

Craig took a step back, sat on a corner of his desk, folded his powerful arms across his broad chest and gave Katy a hard, speculative look. Then he said, "All right, I'm going to tell you only once exactly what the situation with Ronald Crowder is. You can take my word for it or you can take the word of a miserable weakling. That's what Crowder is, you know. A weak man, one of life's failures. Failures like that often cannot live with their own lack of character, so they try to blame somebody else. It's the only way they can live with themselves.

"Ronald Crowder," Craig continued, "is a dope head and an alcoholic. He once had a lot of potential as an actor. But he couldn't leave the bottle alone. He couldn't leave pills and all the rest of it alone. Yes, I had him thrown off the lot of a picture he was to do with me. I'm sure he told you about that. It's common knowledge. The reason? Because he came on the set bombed out of his mind, day after day. He couldn't remember his lines. He was costing us a fortune in retakes. I was patient with the man, up to a point. But I finally had to give him an ultimatum. Either he got straight or he was off the picture and through ever working on a production with me again. Well, he came on the set the very next day, totally spaced out. I was finished with him. Word got around, I suppose. His career took a nose dive. Instead of trying to get his life straightened out, he's developed a persecution complex aimed at me. Somehow in his twisted mind he's blamed me for his own failure."

Katy felt confused and uncertain now. Who was telling the truth—Ronald Crowder or Craig? "He—he says you're going to file charges, have him sent to prison for years."

"You can bet your life on it. He came within minutes of destroying this entire production. I can't allow this to happen again."

"Somehow it makes you seem so heartless—so cruel. I mean, if the man is as messed up as you say, he's sick, isn't he? He needs help—"

Craig rose from his perch on the desk, towering over Katy like a menacing shadow. "I have no sympathy or compassion for a whining weakling. We all have tough things to overcome in life. Anybody can overcome obstacles and make out of his or her life what he wishes, if he's got some character. If a person is a born loser, too weak to overcome his own problems, then he deserves to fail."

The cold steel in Craig Sverenson's voice sent a shiver down Katy's spine. But she gathered enough courage to say, "There is one more thing I have to ask you. Ronald Crowder said that the real reason you had it in for him, aside from professional reasons, was jealousy over your ex-wife, Dolores Ramon. He said there were rumors linking Crowder with Dolores and that was the real reason you had him barred from the lot."

Katy was not entirely prepared for the effect her words had on Craig. For a fleeting second he looked like a man who had been stabbed in the stomach. There was a look of raw pain, a split-second glimpse of a private hell deep within the man and it was instantly hidden behind a dark curtain that slammed shut in his eyes. In a low voice, ominous with warning, he said, "There is one thing I will not discuss with you or any other reporter or any other human being on the face of this earth and that is my personal life with my wife, Dolores."

With that he strode from the office, slamming the door behind him.

Katy stood where he had left her, feeling somewhat like the night she'd gotten lost in the snowstorm—as if she didn't know where she was or where she was going. She was totally confused. It was as if this morning had plunged her into the spinning center of the storm.

One thing Craig had said echoed in her mind like the vibration of a giant bell. ". . . *my wife, Dolores*." Not, my ex-wife, Dolores." ". . . *my wife*—" Was it a slip of his tongue? A slip that revealed how he felt about the beautiful actress, that in spite of the legal divorce, in his heart she was still his wife?

Katy's reaction to that only added to her emotional confusion. She couldn't put her finger on what her reaction was—except that it was basically disturbing, another disturbing emotion added to what had been a most disturbing morning.

Katy left Craig's motor home in a daze. She crossed the camping area, deep in thought, and almost ran blindly into Marsha Trident.

"Hey," Marsha laughed, "have I suddenly become invisible?"

"Oh, Marsha, I'm sorry," Katy apologized miserably. "I just wasn't looking where I was going. This morning has been very upsetting."

Marsha walked beside her. "I take it you've been in town to see Ronnie Crowder, then?"

"Yes. I've talked to him and to Craig. Craig is either a heartless, jealousy-ridden Simon Legree or Ronnie is a dangerous drug addict, depending on which one you want to believe."

Marsha glanced thoughtfully at Katy. "Which one do you believe?"

"Well, I want to believe Craig," she admitted. "But he's acting so darn heartless. If Ronnie is basically a weak person addicted to drugs or alcohol as Craig says, it seems to me that he's a sick person who should have a little sympathy. But Craig apparently has no patience with weakness. He calls Ronnie a weakling, a born loser. He seems to have nothing but contempt for a person who can't cope with life's problems. I gathered he's going to see to it that Ronnie spends a long time in jail."

"Well, Ronnie did almost wreck this film and Craig has a lot at stake here."

"True. I can understand Craig's anger about that. But there's another element in Craig's character that simply eludes me."

"Well, Craig is an actor, after all," Marsha pointed out. "You never know when he's giving a performance. My impression, for what it's worth, is that Craig Svcrenson is actually a private person who puts on his extroverted, blustering act for his public in order to conceal his privacy. He does like an audience and surrounding himself with people. But in the midst of all the crowds Craig keeps a certain private territory of his inner self carefully hidden."

"A very good analysis, Marsha! That would explain why I'm so frustrated, trying to get anything down on paper about Craig that doesn't have an empty, shallow ring. I've never unlocked the door to Craig's private world."

Katy thought about that for a moment, then squared her shoulders resolutely. "Well, I'm not giving up! I'm going to get every person in this movie company cornered, from the script girl to the bit players. I'm going to pick their brains about Craig until I find somebody who has the magic key that unlocks the mystery of Craig Sverenson. Maybe it will be like putting a jigsaw puzzle together: bits and pieces from these different people who have worked with Craig, who are familiar with his moods. One day it will all fall together and I'll have the secret of the real Craig Sverenson."

Remaking the scenes at the pueblo village delayed the company two days. Then they moved down the Rio Grande toward Albuquerque.

Following her resolve, Katy busied herself interviewing the people who surrounded Craig: script writers, make-up persons, actors, cameramen, technicians and that odd assortment of friends and "hangers-on" who somehow attached themselves to superstars like Craig.

The composite picture that grew out of her interviews only made Craig a more complex, enigmatic man. On the one hand he had a reputation for being extremely generous. He never turned down requests to donate his time for charity shows. On some occasions, he had made overseas flights at his own expense to appear in fund-raising events for worthy causes. He was known as the softest touch in the film industry. An actor who was temporarily down on his luck could always get a personal loan from Craig without worrying about a time limit on paying the loan back.

He made friends on an international scale. Included in his close personal friends were a deposed monarch, the chief executive of one of the world's largest automobile manufacturing firms, an ex-vice president, a well-known race car driver who had been a first-place winner at Indianapolis, a heavyweight boxing champion, a professional gambler and a jockey.

He had several homes, a chalet in Switzerland, a condominium on the West Coast and a house in the Bahamas, the latter being his favorite hideaway between films.

He was known for his spontaneous parties. When he was in one of his party moods, he might call friends on another continent and keep the party going until they could fly in to join him. Or he might round up a bunch of extras, bit players and stunt men and women. On more than one occasion he'd been known to call the local Salvation Army, asking them to send over any indigents they were feeding to fill out his party and enjoy the food and festivities.

That was the warm, generous and gregarious side of Craig Sverenson. But he was a paradox for there was another Craig Sverenson who appeared in the interviews Katy conducted, a man who was prone to dark, brooding moods when he preferred solitude. And this darker side of Craig included that element of ruthlessness that bothered her so much, that she had seen in the incident with Ronald Crowder. He seemed particularly scornful of weakness and failure and impatient with mediocrity. When he began a film, he was a relentless slave driver, pushing himself, his film crew and the other actors to the point of nervous exhaustion, demanding that scenes be shot over and over, never totally satisfied with the end results.

And then there was the daredevil macho side of Craig Sverenson, putting his life on the line in high-risk sports such as sky diving, motor cross bike races, hang glider flying and hot air balloon trips. Katy wondered what he was trying to prove with these dangerous activities. Did he have to risk death to conquer his fear of dying? Or was an unconscious death wish a part of that darker side of his soul, seeking death as a friend rather than an enemy?

At last, in a dusty village on the banks of the Rio Grande, not far from Albuquerque, Katy found an important answer to the riddle of Craig Sverenson.

Chapter Seven

His name was Borg Anderson. He was a big, florid-faced Swede with snow-white hair that was kept cropped in a very short burr style. Katy had often heard him yelling at the other cameramen in several languages. She learned that he had been Craig's chief cameraman on all of Craig's films. She had been eager to interview him, especially after hearing that he'd known Craig all his life—was, in fact, almost like family. But Borg was a gruff, impatient man, too busy to talk to her. He'd shooed her away with a growl everytime she had approached him while they were working on location.

She finally caught him in a friendlier mood when the crew stopped in the small New Mexico town for a brief rest.

Craig had followed his characteristic *modus operandi,* keeping the pressure on himself and the film crew until nerves were brittle and tempers were flaring. Then they arrived in the town, Craig became fascinated with a local rodeo and declared a holiday. The film crew gratefully checked into the one motel the town had to offer, happy to be out of tents, trucks and sleeping bags, able to wash off the red dust of New Mexico under hot showers and sleep in real beds.

That day Katy encounted Borg Anderson by chance when she was hunting for a place to have lunch. He was having a hamburger and a pitcher of beer by himself in a booth in the rear of a small dark cafe. The place smelled of frying grease, cigarette smoke and stale beer. A jukebox up front was thumping out the latest country western hit tune.

"Hello," Katy said tentatively. "Mind if I share the booth with you?"

He shrugged. "It's a public place."

Well, at least he didn't run me off, Katy thought, taking heart and sliding into the booth across the table from the taciturn cameraman.

She ordered a hamburger and tried to break the ice by making small talk which, at first, was answered mostly by grunts. But as the level of beer in Borg's pitcher dropped lower, his sociability rose. His grunts became sentences. He yelled at the bartender for a second pitcher of beer. Gradually his gruff exterior melted away, his face became even more florid than normal as the beer loosened his tongue.

Adroitly Katy steered the conversation around to Craig. Her information was correct. Borg hailed from the same small town in Sweden as Craig. He was personally acquainted with Craig's family. He had seen Craig grow to manhood.

"Yah, he was a sickly one, that boy," Borg recalled. "Skinny, pale. Sick with the asthma. Poor family. Not enough money for good medical care. We in the village didn't think that Craig would ever grow to manhood.

114

But that boy had a toughness inside that was twice as strong as his weak body. He prayed hard for God to help him. He's very religious, you know. Not many people know that about Craig. Something he keeps to himself. But he's a man with a strong faith. Maybe that's what helped him. Maybe he just outgrew the asthma. I don't know much about things like that. I just know when he got to be a teenage boy that Craig became a physical culture nut. He climbed the mountains. He slept outside in the cold fresh air. He worked for a grocery store and got plenty to eat. He comes from a family of tall big men. Suddenly he shot up to over six feet. Skinny as a bean pole, for a while, but tough as leather. He started lifting weights, built up his muscles. You see now what a big strong man he is. He learned to love the outdoors. That's his real home. He gets restless like a caged animal when he has to be cooped up in a house too long."

Katy's hamburger lay untouched and forgotten on her plate as she listened with rapt attention, absorbing every word. Here was the key to the real Craig Sverenson, starting with a sickly childhood and an iron will to overcome his handicaps of sickness and poverty. Now, in a blinding flash, she understood his scorn for weakness, his lack of sympathy for failures. "Compensation" was the psychological term—the inner drive that some people had to overcome handicaps, to compensate for physical obstacles in ways that probably made them greater successes than if they had not fought life's battle and won.

"How did he ever become an actor?" Katy asked.

"Born in him, I guess," Borg said. "He was in plays in high school. Then he went off to work in the big cities. When Craig makes up his mind, nothing can stop him. He got jobs with a company that made movies, learned it all from the bottom up, camera, cutting rooms—he knows it all. Then he got small acting parts. First little industrial films. Television ads. Soon bigger parts. You know the rest. Big success. But he didn't forget his people back home in that little village, his family, his friends. No sir. His family isn't poor any-more. They got a nice house to live in. Craig bought it for them. He sent for me. Taught me everything about filmmaking. I've been with him almost from the start. I wouldn't be anything without Craig. I see to it those dumb cameramen do their job right or I break their lousy necks. I love Craig." He was silent for a moment. Then he said quietly, "If he asked me to, I'd die for him."

Katy was deeply touched by this simple, gruff, loyal man, who was Craig's closest friend. Was he perhaps Craig's only real friend? Were all the others acquaint-ances, hangers-on, who would dissolve like the mist if Craig's fame vanished and he turned into just an ordinary man? Not so with Borg, Katy knew with instinctive certainty. This was one of those rare in-stances when one man truly loved another, not in the physical sense but with the kind of bond that drew men close together such as in warfare, when a buddy would sacrifice his life for his friend. It was the classical kind of friendship between two strong, masculine men, a kind of friendship women rarely knew with other members of their own sex.

Her talk with Borg Anderson left Katy in a turbulent state of emotion. For the past week she had been poking and probing into the character of a man who had become a disturbing factor in her life. Now she could put it all together and Craig Sverenson had become achingly human to her, a man of strengths she could admire and weaknesses she could understand.

She could have no more difficulty in writing a revealing, moving article about the man. But what about her own feelings? Craig had become much more than just the subject for an article she was writing. Why try to delude herself? She could no longer be objective about him. She thought about the promise—the *threat*—he had made that she would succumb to him before the journey down the Rio Grande was ended. Now more than ever she was afraid of him, afraid of herself. Nothing she had learned about him reassured her on that score. He remained what he had been since that first moment she had fallen under his spell on the river bank—a man who had it in his power to vanquish her and break her heart in the process. All she had accomplished by getting to know his life better was to make herself even more vulnerable.

When she returned to the motel cabin she was sharing with Marsha, she found her roommate pulling on a clean pair of blue jeans with an air of obvious excitement. "We're all going to the rodeo," she said. "Are you coming along?"

"I don't know," Katy replied. "I really should stay here and get some work done on my article."

"You'll miss some excitement," Marsha warned. "That idiot, Craig, is going to ride a bucking bronco. Isn't that what you Americans call a wild horse?"

Katy's eyes widened. *"What?"*

"You heard correctly, love. Ever since we got in town, Craig has been down at the rodeo grounds, becoming buddies with all the cowboys. Now he's got it in his head that he wants to enter the competition and ride one of the wild horses. Naturally, being Craig Sverenson, he has to have an audience, like a boy showing off, so he's sent word for us to come down and root for him."

117

"The *idiot!*" Katy gasped. "He'll break his fool neck!"

"Very possibly. The producer is having kittens. But nobody can do anything with Craig when he makes up his mind about something. Stubbornest man on the face of the earth!"

Katy hurriedly changed into a fresh pair of blue jeans and a checkered western shirt. Her fingers trembled as she tied a green scarf around her throat. She was both angry and frightened—angry that Craig would do such a foolhardy thing and frightened that he might be seriously injured or even killed. She quickly ran a comb through her dark red hair that she wore in a practical short style, checked her lipstick in a mirror and hurried out with Marsha.

Getting into a company truck, they saw Tony Wilkins emerge from one of the cabins, festooned with cameras, waving at them excitedly. "Give me a ride?" he called.

Katy waited impatiently while he tumbled in beside them. "I just heard Craig's entering the rodeo," he said breathlessly. "I want to get a picture of him falling off a horse."

"Listen, it isn't amusing," Katy said tightly, backing the truck out at breakneck speed. "He doesn't know anything about rodeo riding. It's another one of his adolescent showoff stunts to prove his macho. He's probably going to get hurt."

Tony shrugged. "Well, you want an interesting article, don't you? Our readers would devour pictures of Craig Sverenson being carried off the rodeo grounds on a stretcher. And we'll have the exclusive photos."

"Tony, shut up!" Katy said angrily, blinking uninvited tears away to clear her vision.

"Do be a bit careful, love," Marsha said nervously. "The way you're driving, *we* may be the ones carried off on a stretcher."

A haze of red dust hung over the rodeo grounds. It was an event typical of small southwestern towns. A rough board fence surrounded the area. Bleachers of weathered planks held a motley crowd of townsfolk, Mexican ranch hands, Indians, farmers and construction workers, all sweltering under the hot dusty sun. Most of the spectators wore broad-brimmed hats stained dark with perspiration. They ate hot dogs, quenched their thirst with soft drinks and cheered the riders as barefooted children ran through the crowd and tumbled on the dry grass behind the bleachers. The metallic voice of an announcer over a public address system mingled with the swelling roar of the crowd and the thud of hooves against the churned earth. Periodically an electric horn brayed to indicate a timed ride.

The mingled odors of dust, livestock, perspiring people and cotton candy assailed Katy's nostrils.

Marsha, who had never seen an American rodeo (she pronounced it roh-day'-oh) was enthralled. She asked Katy a barrage of questions, but Katy, who had spent her entire life in Manhattan, was not much better informed and passed the questions on to Tony.

Tony, pronouncing it "roh'dee-oh" as was more commonly done in the Southwest, gave the two women some background information between events. "Most of these rodeos," Tony explained, "include things like wild bronco riding, bulldogging, calf roping, steer roping, bull riding, team roping, wild-cow milking contests, trick riding and trick roping and sometimes, trained horse acts."

"Oh, look, a clown!" Marsha exclaimed, as a comically dressed individual in baggy pants and clown make-up rolled a red-white-and-blue barrel into the arena.

Tony nodded. "That guy might look funny but he's got a serious job. They're going to have the wild steer riding contest next. The rider comes out of that chute," Tony pointed to a heavy wooden gate, "on the back of a mean, bucking Brahma bull, holding onto a rope or leather strap. When the rider gets thrown, there's a good chance that steer will turn around and gore him or tromp him to death. It's the clown's job to run out in front of the steer and get the animal to chase him. Then the clown dives in the barrel for protection. The rider's life can depend on how good the clown is."

Marsha shuddered. "They play bloody rough out here, don't they?"

"Well," Tony said, "ranch life can be rugged. Most of the events you see here today are things that cowboys and cowgirls do on a ranch as every day work. That's how rodeos got started—competitions the cowboys held among themselves after the roundups in the early days."

Tony gave them a brief description of some of the other events they'd see this afternoon. "Bulldogging is where the cowboy, on a horse, rides alongside a bull, jumps from his horse, grabs the bull by the horns, digs his heels in the dirt and twists the bull's neck to wrestle him to the ground. A good bulldogger can throw the bull in less than ten seconds.

"In calf roping, the rider comes out of his chute in hot pursuit of the calf. He ropes the calf with his lariat and ties his end of the rope to his saddle horn. His horse is trained to hold the rope taut while the rider jumps to the ground and ties the calf up with ropes that are called 'piggin' strings.'"

"How come you know so much about it?" Katy wanted to know.

"I spent a summer out West doing a photo series one year. Followed the rodeo circuit for a while," Tony explained.

Katy waited impatiently through the steer riding, calf roping and bulldogging events, too worried to enjoy the spectacle. Then came the announcement that sent a fresh chill through her body. "Ladies and gentlemen," the announcer's voice echoed from the loudspeaker, "today we have a special treat that has come as a big surprise to all of us. The famous European movie star, Craig Sverenson, was passing through our town on his way to shooting his newest film on location here in New Mexico. Craig tells us he's interested in American rodeos. Well, folks, he wants to try his hand at our wild horse riding event. Ladies and gents, Craig Sverenson is mounting his horse in the chute now. He'll be the next performer you'll see—"

A roar of surprised excitement erupted from the crowd.

Katy felt her fingernails digging into her palms. A wave of anger swept through her. What an impossible fool Craig was! A showoff, a crowd pleaser. Risking his neck for a new thrill. Why should she upset herself over the idiot? Let him break every bone in his body. It would serve him right. He deserved no sympathy from her—and wouldn't get any!

The gate to the chute sprang open. The crowd leaped to its feet. Wide-eyed, Katy saw the horse, a huge, furious animal, burst into the arena with maddened leaps. Through a haze of dust Katy caught flashing glimpses of Craig astride the bucking horse. Her breath caught in her throat. Her anger and fright were momentarily forgotten. Craig was a magnificent sight—a big, wide-shouldered, beautiful specimen of manhood engaged in a primitive battle between man and beast to determine who was master. She thought it was like a scene from a Roman coliseum being replayed in modern Western trappings. Craig was the powerful gladiator from a bygone era, pitting his will and strength against a furious animal.

The horse was plunging up and down with arched back and rigid legs, all of its instincts telling him frantically to dislodge the hated man-thing from his back. Craig held the reins with one hand while his other arm swung in the air.

The action lasted only a few seconds that were like a slow-motion sequence in Katy's mind. The horse bucked part way across the arena. Then Katy's horrified eyes saw Craig losing his balance. The next powerful leap of the horse sent Craig crashing to the hard earth.

Another surge of voices from the crowd. Then a hush. Hundreds of eyes were directed to the prone figure of the big man lying still in the dirt. Katy heard a whimper of fright—realized it came from her own throat which she was clutching with an icy hand.

Craig was sprawled out like a broken doll. No sign of life.

Some men were running toward him from the chutes.

Again it was all in slow motion.

Then Katy saw the sprawled figure move, slowly sit up, shake his head. Painfully Craig staggered to his feet. He faced the stand and waved. A great roar of relief answered from the stands and then applause.

The announcer was giving Craig's time on the horse, which Katy later learned wasn't bad for an amateur. But at that moment the announcer's voice was only a blur in her ears, drowned out by the painful thudding of her heart. Her knees gave way and she sat on the hard bleacher. At the moment she was too drained to feel anything. Later her anger at him would return.

The other men reached Craig's side. One of them slapped him on the back, the other pumped his hand. Then Craig limped slowly back to a gate with them.

"I wonder if he broke anything?" Katy heard Marsha ask.

"I wish he'd broken his fool head!" Katy said grimly.

Tony, who had been snapping pictures furiously with a telephoto lens and automatic drive attached to his cameras, now dashed from the stand to get more pictures of Craig in back of the chutes.

The announcer's voice sounded over the loudspeakers again. This time Katy made out his words.

"Folks, here's a bit of news you'll all want to hear. We've just been given word from Craig Sverenson that he's giving a party tonight at the Broken Spur dance hall. He's inviting everyone connected with the rodeo and all the folks from town to come to the party as his guests!"

Whoops and yells greeted the announcement.

"Well, it figures," Marsha said. "I thought it was about time for Craig to get into one of his partying moods. This will be something for you to see, Katy. When Craig works, he works like a fiend. And when he plays, he plays just as hard!"

That evening Katy enjoyed the luxury of a hot shower, soaping herself from head to foot and washing the grime of the rodeo arena dust from her body. She welcomed the biting needles of water turning her bare skin a rosy pink. She turned from side to side, from front to back, letting the tension soak from her muscles under the stinging massage of the water. How marvelous it was to enjoy the comforts of civilization once again! These past weeks she had nearly frozen to death in a snowstorm. She'd been burned by the sun, whipped by the wind. She was sure she'd inhaled a bushel of dust. Insects had stung her. A bear had almost attacked her. Craig could have his great outdoors. It was city life for her!

But then, as her palms slid over the soapy, slippery surface of her body, her flesh remembered the touch of Craig's hands in the secret places now under attack by the stinging water and turned even pinker. She felt an inner heat rising to match the steam that was filling the shower. She closed her eyes and felt again the sweet touch of his mouth on hers. The aching, the tumultuous yearning bubbled up inside her until she was writhing in the sensuous heat of the water.

With a gasp she came to her senses. She grabbed for the shower handles and turned the water to cold as far as it would go. The shock of the icy stream blasted all forbidden thoughts of Craig Sverenson from her mind. Her skin went from pink to white. She forced herself to stand there until her teeth were chattering and she had her head back on straight. Then she turned off the water and stepped, dripping and shivering, from the shower. With a rough bath towel, she restored her body to a healthy pink, rubbing herself dry vigorously.

Western styles would be in order for tonight's party. Katy slipped into wispy undergarments, but from there on it was all drugstore cowgirl. Blue jeans, stitched shirt with pearl buttons and a western hat she'd bought at a store on her way back to the motel.

"I look like a character from the old West," she grinned at herself in the mirror.

The mirror was a painful reminder of her firsthand encounter with the great outdoors. She was sunburned and freckled. It would take a week of intensive care in a beauty shop to restore any luster to her windblown hair. "Redheads," Katy muttered, "are not designed for country life."

"You look adorable to me," Marsha protested. "You have acquired that healthy, outdoorsy, American girl-next-door look."

"What I have acquired," Katy said, "are a bunch of freckles."

"But freckles can be charming. A lot of girls would be delighted to have some."

"Well, they're welcome to mine!" Then Katy said, "And while we're on the subject, you look absolutely stunning, Marsha. You have a great figure for jeans."

The tall willowy English girl was also dressed in western attire. "Well, the boots are killing my feet, but I'm determined to be part of the crowd."

The Broken Spur dance hall was a great wooden building located on the fringe of the small town. There were a few scattered adobe dwellings in the vicinity, but behind the dance hall was open prairie dotted with sagebrush and cacti. Pickup trucks filled the parking area. From the hall came the amplified music of a string band punctuated by whoops and hollers of the crowd.

"Looks like the party's already in full swing," Katy observed. Katy, Marsha and Tony had walked from the motel which was less than half a mile away.

When they entered the dance hall they were engulfed by a tidal wave of humanity. It appeared to Katy that the entire town had accepted Craig's invitation and had brought the whole family. Children were running around the outer fringe of the dancing couples or sleeping on benches against the walls. It was a robust, noisy uninhibited event. When the string band played a rousing version of "Cotton-Eyed Joe," the crowd responded with whoops and yells.

Katy stood on the sidelines with Tony, watching the dancers link arms, form lines and kick heels in the traditional "Cotton-Eyed Joe" dance.

Then the band swung into a western two-step. Tony grabbed Katy, insisting they participate. Katy's dancing experience had been confined to discos, but she bravely joined the fun, managing somehow to keep from being stepped on as Tony whirled her around the floor.

When the dance ended, Katy glanced toward the bar at one end of the dance hall and saw a group of people around a man who towered above the others. "Tony," she said, "there's—there's Craig. I want to try to talk with him for a minute. Okay?"

"Sure," Tony replied. "I'll go see if Marsha wants a lesson in American dancing."

Katy had not spoken with Craig since their encounter in his motor home office over a week ago. As she approached him, she wondered what kind of reception she would get from him—or if he would even speak to her.

She stood on the fringe of the crowd for a few minutes and suddenly he noticed her. "Well," he chuckled, "it's our tenderfoot city girl reporter."

She flushed but was determined not to let him make her angry. "Could I talk with you for a minute?"

"Why not? Suppose we dance. Sounds like the band is playing a waltz. Can you waltz?"

"Not—not very well," she admitted. Her heart gave a skip as she looked up at the broad-shouldered man towering over her. Craig Sverenson's powerful arm went around her waist. She was light-headed, out of touch with reality as he swung her around the dance floor with expert steps. Was there anything he couldn't do well?

Tonight she felt shy and at a loss for words. Finally

she gathered her courage and broke the silence. "I—I wanted to talk to you because I feel I owe you an apology."

He looked down at her quizzically. "An apology?"

"Yes. I'm afraid I was overreacting and . . . well, I was rude when I talked to you that day in your motor home office. I had gotten myself into an emotional state—" She sighed. "Well, the point is, I thought you were being coldblooded, ruthless, cruel, that you were totally lacking in compassion for other people. But . . . the truth is, I've learned some things about you, about your background that I didn't know before. I can understand now why you have little patience for human weakness and failure."

He continued to regard her with a questioning expression. "What has changed your opinion of me so drastically?"

"I made it a point to interview everyone associated with you. Mostly I learned about you from your lifelong friend, Borg Anderson. He told be about the terrible obstacles you had to overcome, the childhood poverty, the health problems. I guess I had to admire you after hearing that story."

Craig looked slightly annoyed. Had she ventured into that sacrosanct private part of his life? But all he did was mutter, "That Borg talks too much. You must have caught him when he was tanking up on beer."

Again they danced in silence. Katy was at a loss to know how he had reacted to her apology.

She decided to change the subject. "Were you hurt when the horse threw you this afternoon?"

Now a slow smile tugged at his lips. "Nothing broken, but every muscle in my body aches."

"Should you be dancing?"

He shrugged. "It's better to keep moving or I'll get

stiff. The town doctor checked me over and gave me some pills for the pain. To tell you the truth, right now I really don't feel anything."

"It was a crazy thing to do—riding a wild horse like that."

"I didn't ride him very long," Craig smiled ruefully.

"Why did you do it?"

"Seemed like a good idea at the time. Fits right into the story we're filming. What would be more natural for the hero in *The Last Adventure* than to encounter a rodeo on his trip down the Rio Grande and decide to try his hand at riding a wild bronco. It's one of the few adventures left in today's artificial world. I think we'll shoot a rodeo scene for the movie."

"You mean you're going to ride a horse like that again?" she asked aghast.

He nodded, a teasing glint in his eye. "A few more times and I may get the hang of it."

"A few more times and you may break your neck."

"Would you mind if that happened, Katy O'Hara?"

She blushed and avoided his eyes. "Of course," she mumbled. "I wouldn't want you to get hurt."

"Seems like a few times since we've met you'd have been delighted if I'd broken my neck."

She had no answer for that.

Craig had maneuvered her through the dancing throng to one of the hall's exit doors. Now he took her hand and led her outside. The sound of the music and dancers faded into the background. Now they were alone with the prairie stretching far away to a distant dark mountain range, and the indigo sky above them was splattered with stars. The parking lot was a sea of cars, metallic surfaces gleaming softly in the starlight.

The tall broad-shouldered man towering over her

blotted out a segment of the stars. "Y'know," he said, continuing to regard her with a teasing, challenging expression, "I do believe, Katy O'Hara, that your heart is beginning to melt. Now wouldn't that be something if you found yourself starting to like me?"

Katy tried but could not answer.

Craig's lips met hers. A shudder ran through Katy. She felt her body melt against his in a warm embrace that set her nerve ends on fire. Her racing pulse blotted out the strains of the western band as the blood made a swooshing sound in her ears. All of her senses reeled with the passion Craig was stirring in her. She forgot where she was—who she was. The pressure of Craig's mouth on hers transported her to a magic realm. The two of them floated on emotional tides, in a current through a timeless sphere where nothing mattered but the sweet yearning that choked her and brought tears to her eyes.

Craig crushed her tightly against his muscular chest. She heard a soft moan escape her lips. She slipped her arms around his neck, curling her fingers in the edge of his hair, her body coming alive with delight at the touch of her skin on his. Goose bumps raced down her arms and legs. She pressed her lips harder on his, welcoming the stinging crush of his kiss. No matter how she tried to get her fill of this man, she couldn't satisfy a longing that opened layer after layer to greater and more urgent depths.

He was big, powerful and overwhelming. He took her breath away. He made her legs tremble from excitement. With her eyes closed, she saw again the stars, but they were a different kind, flashing and shooting. He made her want to abandon all manner of civilized behavior she had known through the years. Her blind impulse here in his arms was to throw caution to the wind and offer herself up for his pleasure, whatever that might be.

All she could imagine right now was the giddy ecstasy of his hands trailing over her flesh, making it burn with fire and desire. A throbbing deep in her body pulsated through her, leaving her breathless and limp. In fact, she was so mesmerized, she only vaguely realized that Craig had vanquished her. She had no will or desire to resist him anymore. He had promised that she would surrender to him before this trip was over. She had not admitted to herself that could happen until now.

Craig lifted his mouth from Katy's and then buried his face in her hair. His hands moved to the small of her back, pressing her close against him and she willingly submitted to his powerful hug. His warm breath across her cheek sent flames leaping in her emotions. She was caught up in a rushing tide of passion unlike anything she had ever experienced in her life. She felt a joyous song singing through her being. She felt alive . . . alive . . . alive. She tingled to the tips of her fingers and toes. She didn't understand it, hadn't asked for it, but she could no more fight it than she could stop breathing. It pervaded every inch of her being and she wallowed in the sheer sensuous delight of being swept up in the strong arms of Craig Sverenson.

She sensed his maleness and her femaleness like the rising crescendo of a great symphony. She knew they were destined to consummate a need for each other that had existed since the first night when they were stranded in the mountain cabin.

His kisses sent a fiery trail to the hollow of her throat. She gasped softly when he opened the top buttons of her shirt. Weakly she tried to resist, but her strength was gone. The night air was cool on her bosom. But his kisses quickly turned her delicate, chilled flesh to burning fire.

When she thought she could bear it no more, he gently buttoned her shirt, kissed her and held her again, tenderly now, as the trembling in their bodies gradually subsided.

No word was spoken but his hand slipped into hers and she squeezed his fingers in answer.

She didn't know yet when or where but they would be together again soon, in the right time and place, and she would no more be able to say "no" to him than to order the wind to change its direction.

She hugged his arm as they walked slowly back into the dance hall. She was unaware of the crowd around them. She saw only Craig. She was looking up at his face, drinking in every line and contour. And she was looking when the change came over his expression like a shadow crossing the sun. She saw a sudden line of pain etched deeply around his mouth, a stricken look in his eyes. His face turned pale.

Her breath stopped in her throat. An icy hand clutched at her bosom. Was he having a fatal heart attack? But his eyes were fixed, riveted on the main entrance doorway across the room.

Katy's gaze shot in that direction. And there, framed in the doorway, was one of the most beautiful women she had ever seen in her life.

Katy recognized her at once. Craig's ex-wife. . . . Dolores Ramon.

Chapter Eight

Dolores Ramon wore a shimmering white silk jump suit that hugged her voluptuous figure with a loving embrace that left few contours to the imagination. It was zipped up the front but the zipper was left open far enough to reveal the shadowy valley between proud breasts. The beautiful actress wore large loop earrings that Katy was certain must be pure gold, plus several diamond encrusted gold bracelets that jangled softly when she moved. She was above average height and the platform soles of her sandals made her appear even taller. Her eyes were luminous black, her complexion the hue of a dusky rose.

Katy was aware of a growing hush spreading through the dancing couples like a spreading epidemic as they became aware of the new celebrity who had arrived in their midst. This would be a night the small rural town would be telling its grandchildren about. Finally the orchestra, which was fiddling and strumming to a frozen crowd, faltered and trickled off to silence.

Dolores, as regal as a queen, gazed around the dance hall as if she had expected the awed silence and would have been surprised at any other reaction. Her eyes were on a searching tour until they found Craig, and then the corners of her luscious mouth tilted in a soft smile.

Craig, still holding Katy's arm, moved toward his ex-wife. Katy would have much preferred to hang back, or better still, to hide in a crack in the floor. But with her arm attached to Craig she had no choice except to accompany him. She wondered afterward if Craig was even aware he was still holding her arm.

Katy had the half hysterical feeling that Dolores was engulfed in a shimmering, star-spangled white cloud, so devastating was the impact of her glamor. Katy compared her own appearance—her freckles, wind-damaged hair, mosquito bites, sunburned nose, drug store cowgirl outfit—and wished desperately she could flee.

But Craig said, "Hello, Dolores," in a quiet voice. And through her drowning waves of self-consciousness Katy heard herself being introduced to Craig's ex-wife, Dolores Ramon, who had often been called the most beautiful woman in the world.

Dolores's black eyes flicked momentarily toward Katy but swung immediately back to Craig. "You're looking wonderful, Craig," she said in a soft husky voice that sent shivers of goosebumps down the spine of every red-blooded man within earshot.

"You, too, Dolores," Craig murmured with a slight bow of his head. "But then, you always do."

Katy's eyes flew to Craig's face. She told herself not to look but she had to and suffered the consequences with bitter heart-wrenching pain. It was obvious to her: Craig was still in love with his ex-wife.

Again that soft intimate smile touched Dolores's red mouth. She looked nowhere but at Craig. Then she moved closer, slipped her arms lightly around his neck and kissed him. "It will be so much fun working with you again, darling."

Katy, who meanwhile had moved aside, now felt a bottomless pit opening beneath her. A few minutes ago she had been sharing a passionate embrace with this man, holding nothing back, letting him know with naked certainty that his prophecy was fulfilled—he had, indeed, conquered her. She had not spoken the words aloud, but her heart cried them with each vibrant thud, "I love you . . . I love you—"

What a fool she had been she thought now with bitter shame and remorse, to fall into that age-old trap that has broken the hearts of countless women since time began—to let herself fall in love with a man and to surround him with such an aura of her own love that she imagined he loved her in return.

Now, seeing them together, this utterly exquisite woman and this rugged handsome man, she plunged the knife deeper into her heart, picturing them as man and wife, their bodies locked in flaming love-making, imagining his whispered words of love and her gasping exclamations of passion.

She mumbled some kind of excuse and fled the scene of her agony, certain that Craig wasn't even aware she had gone. Blindly she threaded her way through the gaping crowd and stumbled her way back to the motel where she hid in the dark and soaked a pillow with her tears.

Fortunately she was left with one grain of pride: she had done her crying and washed her tear-stained face by the time Marsha returned. She was in bed in her nighty when the lock in the front door turned and her roommate came in.

"Sorry, Katy," Marsha murmured, flicking on one of the softer lamps. "Did I wake you?"

"No," Katy mumbled, pretending to be half asleep. "I wasn't quite asleep yet. Is the party over?"

"Hardly. Craig's parties rarely end before dawn. You left early."

"I was tired." She hesitated, then was unable to keep from asking, "Is Dolores still at the party?"

"Oh, she signed some autographs, then she and Craig went off somewhere together to discuss the film."

Another knife ripped through her heart. How often was this going to happen? Were Dolores and Craig really discussing the film or were they having a passionate reunion? She knew that some divorced couples were still physically attracted to each other even if they couldn't stand to live together. And the air had sizzled when Dolores's gaze locked with Craig's tonight.

"That was quite an entrance she made, wasn't it?" Marsha observed.

"Yes. I suppose that happens wherever she goes."

Marsha was gazing at her in the soft light from the single lamp. She came over and sat on the edge of the bed, an expression of concern on her face. She chewed on her bottom lip, then ventured, "Once, when we were talking, you said, quote, 'It's none of your business.' Is it none of my business now—or would you feel better if you talked about it?"

"Whatever do you mean?" Katy asked, dangerously on the verge of tears again.

"Well, I would say that you have the look of a woman who has either just flunked her electrocardiogram . . . or saw her love affair go down the tubes tonight."

"That obvious, huh?"

Marsha nodded soberly.

"Well," Katy mumbled, "my electrocardiogram is okay, unless those things register a broken heart." She couldn't hold back a tear that trickled a winding path down her left cheek. "I really made a fool out of myself tonight, Marsha."

The English make-up girl sighed. "It's Craig, isn't it? I've been sensing the vibrations."

"You did warn me," Katy murmured, tears continuing to burn her eyes. "But I thought I was immune to Craig Sverenson—"

Marsha squeezed her hand sympathetically. "Not many women could be immune to a man like that."

"Including his ex-wife. The way they were looking at each other—I think she wants him back. And I'll bet all she'd have to do to get him would be to wiggle her little finger. He's still in love with her—it's obvious." Katy said bitterly, the words, when spoken aloud, giving her heart another painful wrench.

"I don't know," Marsha said slowly, shaking her head in a gesture of puzzlement. "Nobody really knows what Craig is thinking or feeling. I did know there was going to be emotional fireworks when Dolores joined the company . . . as I told you."

Yes, Katy thought, her heart breaking, *but you didn't tell be I was going to be the victim. . . .*

The film company remained in the small New Mexico town for several days, filming some rodeo scenes. Then they resumed the journey down the Rio Grande toward the border of Texas and the wild scenery of the Big Bend National Park.

Katy had not spoken to Craig since the night Dolores had joined them. He was back in his intense mood, preoccupied with the story. And whenever Katy saw him Dolores was at his side.

In the movie story Craig was to meet Dolores in a small town near the Texas border. The location people had arranged for scenes to be filmed in the town, at a gas station, a bar and in a small frame house. Dolores played the part of a young widow who is romantically involved with a local man until Craig meets her and they fall in love at first sight. The local man, a heavy in the story, picks a barroom fight with Carig, loses the fight and later pursues him down the river planning to kill him.

The fight was staged in the local bar. By now Katy was convinced that Craig did not use a stand-in or a stunt man for the dangerous sequences. She had seen with her own eyes that he played the parts himself. But she wished he had used a stand-in for the love scene with Dolores Ramon. It was a torrid scene, shot in the frame house. Dolores, scantily clad, melted in Craig's arms in a searing kiss.

Katy watched the filming of the scene with burning agony. After that she stayed in her tent, working on her article, avoiding any contact with Craig.

She seriously considered catching a plane at El Paso and returning to New York. She knew her editor had instructed her to stay with the film crew until the final scenes were made, but she could probably convince Mike that she had enough material for an in-depth article about Craig Sverenson.

But fighting the cowardly part of her heart that wanted to flee was her reporter's instinct which sensed a new development in the story of Craig Sverenson. If this film brought Craig and Dolores back together, as it appeared to be doing, it would make a powerful addition to her article and a scoop as well. Mike would have her head on a platter if she chickened out and left, missing such an important development. And even stronger than her editor's wrath were her own professional standards. She couldn't turn her back on a story, no matter how her heart was breaking. She had to see this through.

The filming crew set up camp on the edge of the Big Bend National Park. Here they were surrounded by some of the most primitive desert scenery Katy had yet encountered. Gargantuan boulders, sheer canyons, jagged mountains gave her a feeling of insignificance that was awesome and frightening.

They were in a desert region of cactus, thorny shrubs and countless arroyos. When the west was still a raw frontier, men had spoken of this area as the *despoblado,* "the unpeopled place," where only Indians roamed. Little had changed. From where the Rio Grande entered Big Bend National Park until it reached the town of Langtry where Judge Roy Bean once held forth with his "Law West of the Pecos," the river swirled unhampered and wild, at times between canyon walls 1,500 feet deep. On the Texas side were a few arid ranches. Fences were scarce. It was a sunbaked land where buzzards wheeled silently in the cloudless sky. On the Mexican side of the river, a scattering of people lived in a few dusty villages.

Katy stood on the bank of the river. Here the banks were low and the river was narrow. A family of Mexicans dressed in straw hats, sandals and the loose-fitting white garments of the working class, watched curiously. Katy waved and they gravely waved back.

"It's almost as if the river were a boundary between today and the past," a voice said behind her shoulder.

138

Katy turned quickly, catching her breath.

Craig was puffing on his pipe thoughtfully, gazing at the people on the other side of the river. "They'll go home tonight to an adobe hut with dirt floors, lighted with a kerosene lamp and eat tortillas made with corn ground by hand in a stone dish and talk about the strange things the Americanos are doing on this side of the river. Here we are with our twentieth century camera gear, trucks, generators, boats. Cross the river and time slips back a century."

"Mexico is as industrialized and modern as we are," Katy said testily, back on the defensive with him.

"Oh, yes, in certain parts. In the cities. Not in the adobe villages across the river in this area." His brown-flecked green eyes swung in her direction. A shudder ran through her. She felt impaled on his gaze. She fought down a tumult of emotions, remembering with a heart-wrenching pang another time he had found her on a bank of this same river in another state, the first time she had felt herself slipping under the bitter-sweet magic of his spell.

He said, "I haven't seen much of you lately. Have you been hiding?" His tone was gently reproving.

Nervously she wiped her palms on her jeans. "You've been very busy. The picture . . . Dolores—" She floundered.

She wished he'd stop looking into her eyes. When he did that, her mind spun off in a hundred different directions at once. What was he thinking? She could find no answer in his eyes. There was a strained feeling between them this evening. Was it the specter of Dolores Ramon? Of course, she thought.

He said nothing about her mention of Dolores. Instead his gaze turned to the river again. He puffed thoughtfully on his pipe. The aromatic tang of the tobacco touched her nostrils.

"I'm taking a canoe down the river tomorrow," he said, talking around the pipe stem clamped between his strong white teeth. Then he held the pipe in his hand and looked at her again. Now she detected a teasing glint in his eyes. "Want to come along, city girl? I'll show you some scenery you'll never forget."

"In a canoe? In that God-forsaken region?" She waved a hand in the direction of the rugged mountainous terrain. "Through rapids and heaven knows what else? No thank you."

"I didn't think so. Didn't think a city-spoiled tenderfoot would have the nerve," he taunted softly.

Her eyes blazed. "Don't you call me spoiled!" she flung back at him.

"No?" He raised an eyebrow. "Not spoiled by taxicabs and air conditioning and elevators and electric typewriters and computers?" He gazed at the river, as if looking at a distant scene. "Those gadgets wouldn't be much use to you out here, tenderfoot."

If he used that hated sobriquet to provoke her, he succeeded. Stung by his words, too angry to think clearly, she blurted out, "Just because I've lived in the city all my life doesn't mean I'm a coward, Craig Sverenson. I'm not afraid of the river or a canoe trip. I don't like it, but I'm not afraid."

He shrugged. "No, I shouldn't have asked you. You'd probably fall out of the canoe. I'd waste a lot of time fishing you out of the river—"

He turned as if to leave. But she caught his arm, feeling the powerful ripple of his muscles under his shirt. "I take that as a challenge! You're not going to get out of it that easy. You invited me and I'm going.

I'll show you a city girl can be just as brave as a big, loud-talking showoff like you, Craig Sverenson!"

He glanced at her with the teasing glint in his eyes, a smile pulling at his lips. "Very well. Be ready to leave early in the morning."

Only after he had walked away did she fully realize what she had impulsively gotten herself into. A canoe trip down this wild, desolate river. She remembered the night the grizzly bear had given her the fright of her life. What kind of new terrors awaited her in the deep canyons and white water rapids of this primitive stream?

Her heart sank. She was furious with him! He had tricked her into demanding to go with him. But she was more furious with herself. And she knew her pride wouldn't allow her to back out now.

Then she asked herself, why had Craig Sverenson asked her to go with him? The answer came to her at once. As usual when he pulled one of his showoff stunts he wanted an audience. The glamorous Dolores Ramon was not about to spoil her hair style and pampered complexion on a sunburned, wet, miserable trip down the river. So Katy was his second choice. His ego needed constant feeding, she thought angrily, and she had been picked to do the feeding. She would be his adoring audience and write about another of his daring exploits, a firsthand witness.

She felt used and angry at the situation, yet frustrated at trying to find a way out.

Word soon spread around the camp. Tony was worried about the dangers involved and also exhibited a normal amount of masculine jealousy at her going alone on a trip down the river with Craig Sverenson. He and Marsha tried to talk Katy into backing out. But she was stubbornly determined to go through with the ordeal.

Katy slept restlessly that night. She had dreams of falling in the river and being swallowed by a huge snake.

The next morning she rose early and donned moccasins, blue jeans and a white shirt with the tail gathered up and knotted under the third button to leave her midriff bare.

She had no appetite for breakfast. She left the tent, walking slowly toward the river with the feeling of a condemned person going to the gallows.

The film crew and actors had been busy since dawn, shooting some outdoor scenes in the desert near the river. A woman moved away from the group toward Katy. It was Dolores Ramon.

Katy didn't recognize the glamorous star at first. Obviously Dolores was made up for the outdoor scene. She wore a dusty shirt and jeans. A smear of grime had been artfully applied to her left cheek. Her hair was windblown. With it all she managed to look even more beautiful.

"Miss O'Hara, could you spare me a moment?"

"Yes, Katy said, pausing.

Dolores moved closer. She was smiling but her gaze was studying Katy with a woman's meticulous appraisal. "I understand you are going to accompany Craig on his trip through the Big Bend."

Katy nodded.

"I applaud your bravery and wish you luck. I'm only sorry I couldn't go with Craig. He asked me, you know, but we have these scenes to shoot today." She waved a hand toward the cameras. "In this part of the story I'm supposed to have ridden all night to warn him of a man who is following him to kill him. I've ridden to be with the one I love." She smiled again. "Since Craig told me you are writing an article about him and about this film for *Personality Magazine,* I thought you might like to know that making this picture has brought Craig and me together again. It's a wonderful story with dramatic love scenes. I don't have to act or pretend when I play the scenes with Craig. The movie is going to be a smash hit and when we've finished making it, Craig and I will be together again—permanently. That's a bit of exclusive news for your magazine."

Katy's mouth felt as if it were filled with ashes. "Thank you for the information, Miss Ramon," she managed to say.

"Well, good luck again. We'll be in Langtry to meet you and Craig when you reach that point in the river." She smiled again and went back to where the film crew was waiting.

Katy continued toward the river, blinking hard to clear the tears from her vision. She was not taken by surprise by Dolores's little bombshell. It only confirmed what she suspected. But hearing it from Craig's ex-wife gave it a finality that hurt. It was obvious why Dolores had chosen this moment to give her the news. She wasn't overjoyed at Katy going on a canoe trip unchaperoned with Craig and wanted it clearly understood that Craig was once again her property.

"You needn't worry, Miss Ramon," Katy murmured through clenched teeth. "He's all yours. I'll never make a fool of myself over that man again."

But that didn't take away the heartbreak. She'd have *that* to live with for a long time to come . . . perhaps the rest of her life.

She drew a deep breath, swallowed hard, squared

her shoulders, and walked the rest of the way with her chin raised. Craig would never know how her heart was crying over him.

A small knot of people was at the river's edge, helping Craig load the canoe.

"Good morning," he said cheerily in a voice that echoed across the river. "So you didn't back out."

"No, did you think I would?" she demanded, her eyes defiant, her chin raised.

He merely chuckled. He appeared to be in a good mood this morning, anticipating the adventure that lay ahead of them, Katy surmised.

"I don't suppose you've ever ridden in a canoe," he began—a statement more than a question. "Sit upright and don't try to stand. Canoes tip over easily. If we are in the rapids and you go overboard, try to point your toes in the direction the current is carrying you so you don't bash your head on the rocks. Here—" he tossed her a vest-style life jacket.

"I can swim," she protested.

He smiled. "Ever try to swim in white water rapids?"

She put the life jacket on.

Craig helped her into the canoe. Why did the strength of his powerful arms still make her shiver? Part of her wanted nothing more to do with him. Still, her traitorous body quivered at his touch and yearned for more.

The canoe was packed with drinking water, food and survival gear. Katy settled in the prow. Craig took his place at the other end of the aluminum craft with surprising balance and ease for such a huge man. He dipped an oar in the water and the canoe swung easily out into the current.

Katy looked back and saw that Tony and Marsha had come down to see them off. Marsha waved. Tony was busy snapping pictures. But he looked up from his camera and Katy felt a stab of guilt and remorse at the look of anguish that crossed his face. If he only knew how she felt about Craig Sverenson, he could stop being jealous over her taking this canoe trip!

The current carried them swiftly around a bend. The camp disappeared. They were suddenly alone in a great wilderness.

"This is a little late to ask," Katy said, "but why, exactly, are you taking this trip?"

"I want to scout the river, to pick the spots we'll film. I've sent crews overland to meet us up ahead. We'll make it through Santa Elena Canyon today and meet one of the trucks about sundown."

Katy was relieved that she wouldn't have to spend the night alone with Craig somewhere in this awful wilderness.

"Of course you had to take a canoe," she remarked with a degree of acidity. "An inflatable raft would have been much safer."

"But duller. And a canoe is more maneuverable."

Green trees, brush and grass fringed the river for a few yards but beyond lay the harsh brown desert covered by mesquite, creosote bushes and cactus. Craggy mountains rose dramatically from the desert floor, combining with the river to create the stupendous chasms that lay ahead of them.

Once they glided past a lone horseman on the Mexican side, a big-hatted *vaquero*, who gazed at them with solemn dignity and said, *"Buenos días,"* as they passed him.

"Doesn't he look magnificent up on that knoll?" Craig said. "Wish I could hire him for a part in the film."

Katy had relaxed somewhat, her anxiety lulled by the

warm sunlight and the murmuring rhythm of the river. They had encountered no rough water. Perhaps it was going to be a pleasant journey after all.

The painful element was seeing Craig so near, watching the ripple of muscles in his powerful forearms, his broad shoulders straining at his shirt as he guided the canoe with expert skill, all the while realizing she would never know the ecstasy of being loved by him.

Time seemed suspended. She remembered the curious feeling she had had about Craig, that he was a displaced person, a man of an earlier, more robust, unhampered era who had stumbled into the twentieth century by mistake. Right now she had the strange sensation that a time warp had placed them back in that earlier century. He looked so at ease in this primitive environment, a bronzed adventurer, pitting his skill and powerful muscles against the elements. They were completely alone and isolated in this wilderness, just the two of them under the vast sky. Even the one human they had seen since leaving camp, the *vaquero*, was like a figure out of the past.

"You like being in this kind of place, don't you?" Katy suddenly asked, breaking a comfortable silence that had lasted nearly an hour.

"Yes—it's pleasant here. Don't you like it?"

She glanced around at the awesome expanse of harsh unrelenting desert, the brooding mountains, the rugged terrain and she felt a shiver race through her body. "It's pretty frightening to me. I'd hate to get lost out here."

He laughed. "And yet you feel safe in the city where there are cars to run you down, criminals to rob you and poisoned air to breathe."

"Well . . . I suppose those are dangers I'm familiar

with. This is all so strange out here. I know how to deal with traffic, smog and muggers. I wouldn't know how to cope with the desert."

Craig nodded in the direction they were going. "Take a look ahead."

Katy was seated with her back to the prow. She had to twist around to see ahead. When she did, she gasped. They were approaching the maw of a gigantic canyon. It was like the jaws of the mountain opening to swallow them. Next she heard the ominous rumble of rapids. She turned to look at Craig with an expression of panic.

"Relax," he smiled. "Get on your knees and face the front of the canoe. Hold onto both sides. Sit still and balance the boat."

"And pray," she added, trying to keep her teeth from chattering.

They plunged into the rapids with sudden breakneck speed. Foaming water sprayed in Katy's face. All around her the river seethed and boiled over cruel, half-submerged boulders. They shot through narrow gaps between the rocks, sometimes scraping bottom. Katy's heart pounded. Her blood raced through her body with the speed of the river. She felt both terrified and exhilarated as adrenalin pumped into her veins. The thundering river was deafening.

Then they were past the rapids at the mouth of the canyon and into an area of smooth water. Katy sank down, all her muscles limp. After the deafening roar of the rapids, a contrasting silence fell over the river. The canyon walls shut out the wind and plunged them into deep shadows. There was only a narrow slice of blue sky far above them.

She turned to face Craig again. The spraying water

had soaked his shirt, gluing it to the bulging muscles of his shoulders and deep chest. His face was flushed, his eyes bright.

"How did you ever get us through that awful place without wrecking the canoe?" she marveled.

He grinned, white teeth flashing. "That wasn't so bad. We'll be going through worse rapids up ahead."

"Oh, wonderful," she said grimly.

She gazed around at the sheer walls that plunged straight down into the moving river. "How do you propose to ever get a camera crew down here?"

"We'll have some cameramen come through here on inflatable rafts to get action shots of the river. Further along, we should come to some banks. I think we can land cameras there by helicopter. That's one of the things I want to check on."

"How long will we be in this canyon?"

"Probably the rest of the day."

They had a lunch of nuts, dried fruits and granola, without stopping.

At mid-afternoon, Katy heard once again the roar that warned of dangerous rapids up ahead. She crouched in the prow of the canoe, bracing herself for another terrifying ordeal.

As they approached the boulder-strewn white water, she could see this was going to be much worse than the first experience. Jammed between some of the rocks were carcasses of canoes that had not made it.

Once again spray dashed in her face. Once again the slender silver canoe raced between the rocks as water churned around them. Once again her ears were deafened by the current's thunder that reverberated from the canyon walls.

The canoe rocked dangerously. Katy heard Craig shout but she couldn't make out his words. There was a shuddering crash as they bounced off a huge rock. Katy screamed, losing her balance.

Suddenly she felt herself being hurled through the air. She plunged into the water, came up gasping for breath. The river was suddenly a cruel giant with the powerful current turned into grasping hands that yanked her this way and that, hurling her over the rough bottom, bruising her on the giant rocks. She floundered helplessly, trying to keep her feet in the direction of the current to prevent her head from being smashed against the boulders.

The battering seemed to go on forever. She was half drowned. Then a strong arm was around her, dragging her from the dangerous current into a pool of calmer water. Craig swam to the bank, pulling Katy with him. They collapsed on the dry sand, lying there until they had caught their breath.

Katy struggled to a sitting position, realizing that the life jacket and Craig's strong arms had saved her life. "Where is the canoe?" she cried.

Craig propped himself on an elbow and gazed rue fully at the river. "Smashed to pieces and a quarter of a mile downstream by now, I'd imagine."

Katy's face suddenly grew red. "And it's my fault. You'll never let me forget this—"

He shrugged lazily. "I don't think I can entirely blame you. I was losing control of the boat. When you tipped us over, it was just the last straw."

"You don't seem all that concerned!"

He rolled over on his back, gazing up at the sky. "Why should I be? We're alive, aren't we?"

"Yes, but we're stranded here—in this God-forsaken place with no food, no shelter," she wailed.

He grinned at her. "We seem to be making a habit out of getting stranded together in remote places. First that night in the cabin in Colorado. Now on the banks of the Rio Grande. D'you suppose fate is trying to tell us something?"

"Your nonchalance in the face of this crisis," she said heatedly, "is maddening! How do you propose to get us out of this mess?"

He folded his hands behind his head, his brown-flecked green eyes making a lazy survey of their surroundings. "Let's see now. Not being a human fly, I can't climb that sheer canyon wall. This is just a narrow strip of beach with river on all sides, so I can't walk for help. And not being a fish, I can hardly swim for assistance. Guess we're stuck here."

"You don't have to be so darn casual about it! We'll starve to death. Years from now somebody will find our skeletons."

"Entwined, I hope, like Quasimodo and Esmerelda in *The Hunchback of Notre Dame*. That would be romantic, wouldn't it?"

She threw a handful of sand at him.

He merely chuckled at her panic, further infuriating her and bringing her close to tears. Then, as if deciding to take pity on her, he said, "Things aren't quite that desperate. When we don't show up, eventually someone will come looking for us."

"That could take days," she pointed out. "You told me this canyon is miles long. If they send a plane out looking for us, we'd be hard to spot way down here in the shadows of these canyon walls. We could be very hungry by then. And it gets cold in this desert region at night."

"You have a point," Craig admitted. "Let's see what the situation has to offer us." He sat up, clasping his hands around his knees as he gazed thoughtfully at their surroundings. "We're on a sandy bank about fifty feet wide with the canyon wall on one side and the river on the other. It's kind of like a sandbar a hundred or so feet long. That's our prison." Then he nodded toward one end of the bank. "We're in luck over there. I see a bunch of driftwood piled up. Fuel for a campfire."

Katy felt a small glimmer of relief. At least they could keep warm at night. "Then you have some matches?"

He shook his head.

"But how—"

He reached in his pocket. "I have a pocket knife. The only thing salvaged from our shipwreck."

She looked at him with a puzzled expression.

He rose and walked over to the pile of driftwood. Katy followed, watching him curiously.

Craig selected several small pieces of driftwood. With his sharp knife he carefully made a little pile of shavings which he placed on a flat board. He found a straight stick about the size and length of an arrow and scraped it smooth with his knife. Then he squatted before the pile of shavings, held the rod-like stick between his flat palms with one end thrust into the shavings against a small indention in the board. He began twirling the stick rapidly by moving his palms back and forth. "Tell me, Katy," he said, "are you beginning to feel a bit like Robinson Crusoe?"

"More like an Indian squaw watching her brave start a fire." The implication of her words were past her lips before she realized what she'd said and she blushed furiously. Quickly she added, "That *is* the way Indians made fire, isn't it?"

"Sort of. I think they had a more efficient way of doing it by looping the string of a bow around the stick and sawing it back and forth. They could do it faster that way. It works on the principle of friction. The point of the stick twirling in an indention in the board begins to heat up after a while. With some luck the shavings will catch on fire."

He fell silent, working patiently and energetically at his task.

Minutes went by. Nothing happened. Katy said, "It isn't going to work."

"Spoken like a true twentieth-century, city-bred girl," Craig observed. "Turn on the microwave oven and have dinner in ten minutes. Switch on the TV and see a complex life situation solved in thirty minutes. You see, my girl, the people who used to make fire this way were not attuned to the instant gratification of your industrialized world. If it took all morning to get a fire started, that was all right. They had no quartz digital watches reminding them of the minutes ticking away."

Katy rested her chin on her knees, watching Craig doggedly twirl the stick. That world he had spoken about—her world—the world of subways, rush hours and automobile horns seemed very distant—two thousand miles and another century away.

Suddenly her eyes widened. "Look!" she squealed. "It's smoking."

He nodded. "Blow on it. Gently."

She bent over the tiny wisp of smoke curling up from the twirling stick and carefully blew into the pile of shavings. Racial memories stirred in deep layers of her subconscious. She was taking part in a fire-making ritual as old as the days of a cave man and his woman.

She felt tense with excitement as tiny red spots began to appear in the curled ends of the shavings. An exclamation of triumph escaped her lips as the shavings burst into flames. Quickly Craig fed a small stick to the embryo fire, then another and another, working up to

larger pieces of driftwood. Presently they had a respect-
able campfire ablaze.

"That's incredible!" Katy exclaimed, regarding Craig
with a new measure of respect.

"Now," Craig said, "let's see what the river has to
offer us in the way of dinner."

He poked around the driftwood until he found
something that satisfied him, a slender stick about four
feet long. With his knife, he sharpened one end of the
stick.

Katy sat watching as Craig prowled the edge of the
river bank, searching the quiet pools of water around
rocks and logs with sharp eyes. Again she was struck by
the infinite patience he exhibited—the patience of a
hunter stalking his prey.

The narrow strip of blue sky far above them was
turning purple. The shadows at the base of the canyon
walls were growing darker. Katy's stomach felt the
gnawing of hunger pangs, but she was becoming resigned to staying hungry that night. At least, she
thought, the campfire would keep them warm.

Then she saw a flurry of activity. Craig, ankle deep in
the water, had suddenly plunged his crude spear into a
pool under a log. He swung the spear out of the water.
There was the flash of a wriggling fish impaled on the
spear. Craig tossed it on the bank.

"That's a nice, big blue channel catfish, one of the
best tasting freshwater fish you'll find," Craig grinned.
"He was dozing under that log."

Katy marveled at the survival skills of this remark-
able man. He arranged a flat rock in the bed of coals
from their fire. With his pocket knife, he filleted the fish
and broiled it on the rock over the coals.

Soon Katy was hungrily devouring broiled catfish.

"Sorry I can't offer you any salt or lemon for your fish," Craig said, watching with amusement as she ate.

"Ummm," she murmured, licking her fingers that were serving as cutlery. "That has to be, without doubt, the most absolutely delicious meal I have ever eaten in my life."

He smiled. "That's because you're hungry. The ducking you took in the river plus this clean, fresh desert air gave you an appetite."

"It certainly did. Thank you for an unforgettable dinner." She felt her cheeks grow warm as she said impulsively, "You're—you're taking very good care of me."

"Are you still frightened?"

She gazed at him and slowly shook her head. "No. Not any more. Not with you here. You—you seem so at home in this wilderness, so capable. How did you ever learn such survival skills?"

He shrugged. "It's what I do best," he said simply. "The wilderness is my home. I don't feel like an alien here. I do when I'm in the cities."

"We come from two entirely different worlds," Katy said. "Perhaps even from different centuries. We're strangers."

"Are we, Katy O'Hara?" he asked, his eyes, the strange mixture of the brown and green wilderness he loved, gazing at her thoughtfully.

"Yes," she said, growing nervous and avoiding his eyes.

"Perhaps it's a matter of fulfilling the old cliché— opposites attract."

She shook her head, not wanting to trust her voice.

It had grown dark in the canyon and the night chill of the desert was in the air. But their campfire kept her warm. In the narrow band of sky far above, stars twinkled. It was a setting from the Garden of Eden, when the world was young and the touch of God was fresh on the mountains, the valleys and the rivers. At this moment Katy felt the veneer of civilization slipping away. She felt a very basic and primitive femaleness responding to this strong, capable male companion, with his muscles and his wit protecting her from the dangers of the night around them.

She felt very vulnerable. She felt frightened of her own emotions.

His arm went around her. The strength of his steel-like muscles made her tremble.

He murmured her name softly, then kissed her.

Liquid fire flowed through her veins.

The kiss moved to the hollow of her throat. Gently he unbuttoned her shirt. Kisses found the delicate hollows under her collarbone and trailed to her bosom where they ignited twin fires.

Katy's senses were reeling. Her sanity was slipping over the edge of a cliff as the few rational thoughts she had left clawed at the edge to hold on.

He opened his shirt now and embraced her. She felt her naked breasts squeezed against the hairy muscular texture of his chest.

How lovely it would be, she thought, simply to let go now, to close her eyes and sink into the velvet world of sensation and emotion. The throbbing of her heartbeat murmured, "Surrender . . . surrender . . . surrender—"

But a vestige of rational thought held her back. The image of the lovely Dolores Ramon swam into her disorganized mind, bringing a sudden chill and centering of her thoughts. The words Dolores had spoken to her this morning were replayed: "When we've finished making this movie, Craig and I will be together again—permanently. . . ."

That same element of rational thought cautioned her that Craig wanted her for now, for tonight only. He was a virile lusty man, alone in the wilderness and hungry for a woman. A night of love with her, here on this lonely beach, would be no more than a physical act for him. After they were rescued he'd forget about her upon seeing the dazzling Dolores whom he still loved. Just as Katy had been his second choice for this canoe trip, taken along to satisfy his ego, now she would be used to satisfy his male hunger for a female body.

But even with those cold facts chilling the fire in her veins, the temptation remained. They were alone here—as alone as on another planet. Why not take the pleasures the night offered? Why not close her mind to reason, give in to her passion . . . and have at least this night to remember?

Who would ever know?

The answer was obvious and painful: She would know.

No, her cautious self warned, drawing back from the dangerous but inviting chasm. The few hours of insanity would not be worth the lifetime of heartbreak they would leave. She didn't need any more piognant memories of Craig to torment her. What she needed was less contact with him. She needed to begin the healing process and the sooner the better. A night in his arms followed by wrenching separation might leave her with a depression she couldn't survive.

She turned her face away from his kisses. In an unsteady voice she whispered, "Please, Craig, I don't want to go any further. I'm not being coy or teasing. I really don't want to."

He drew back, his expression more puzzled than frustrated. He searched her face. "But the way you kissed me that night at the dance hall after the rodeo. I thought—"

"I know. That wasn't fair to you. It wasn't fair to me. I'm not the kind to lead a man on, Craig, or to tease. I—well, I wasn't thinking straight that night. Things have changed since then and . . . well, it would be a mistake, now . . . something I'd regret."

She reached over and laced her fingers in his. "Craig, I'm certainly tempted. This setting—the river, the stars, the campfire, alone here with you. It would drive any woman out of her mind."

The campfire was casting flickering light and shadows playing over his rugged features. She touched his face with a finger that trembled. "Yes," she whispered huskily, "I would like for you to make love to me. I'm not a cold woman at all. And you're a devilishly attractive man. As if your ego hadn't already told you that," she laughed softly. "Maybe that's part of your charm—that male ego that makes you so sure of yourself, so confident of your own ability, your own maleness. Women have a weakness for confident, self-assured men. At least I do."

"But still you say 'no' to me." Craig thought for a moment, then said, "That night in the Indian pueblo in New Mexico. I wasn't spying on you but I couldn't help seeing that you kissed Tony Wilkins, the photographer from your magazine. Are you in love with him?"

"Tony and I have an unspoken understanding," she replied. She nodded slowly. "Yes, Tony loves me and I care for him. We'll probably wind up getting married when we return to New York. And on your side of the picture, there's your ex-wife, Dolores. It's obvious to me that there is still a lot of caring between you." She wanted to tell Craig that she knew he and Dolores would be resuming their marriage. But she felt if she did Craig would know how she truly felt about him and how much she hurt.

Craig didn't reply but she saw that look of anguish she'd seen before cross his face. No doubt Dolores had broken his heart once. But he was ready to forgive and take her back. The fact that he made no reply was answer clear enough.

"She's a beautiful, beautiful woman," Katy said softly. "And I can understand how you feel about her. . . ."

"You don't understand fully, Katy O'Hara, because I don't understand fully myself. . . ."

Tears burned Katy's eyes. "But I *do* understand," she whispered, "that there are other people involved. So help me pass the night, Craig. Talk to me and protect me and keep me from being afraid. But . . . please . . . don't make love to me."

She saw a scowl on his face, the expression of a man who had been sexually aroused, only to have his natural instincts frustrated. In a small voice she said, "We're alone here . . . I—I suppose you could force me to submit. But would you want to have me that way, Craig?"

He shook his head slowly. "That's not my idea of how to conquer a woman. I told you when we first met that one day you'd surrender. But I meant you'd come to me willingly."

And I would. Oh, I would, if only you truly loved me. If only it were me instead of Dolores holding the key to your heart. . . .

But she didn't put her thoughts into words. Instead they sat beside the fire in silence as it burned down into glowing coals. Finally Craig rose and walked off into the darkness to gather more wood. He piled enough nearby to see them through the night and fed some logs to the coals to keep the fire going.

When there was enough blaze for Katy to see his face, she could tell the passion was gone.

After a while they began talking again. Craig got off on tales of his adventures. Katy was entertained and entranced. He was a marvelous storyteller. She was the audience he craved. He told about his first experience with a hang glider, flying from a cliff in California. "I went straight up in the air and then straight into the ocean. The second time I sort of got the hang of it. Before the day was over I was pretty good at it."

They both laughed. Then he launched into a long, amusing story about a movie he filmed in Paris. "There was a huge banquet scene. The director insisted on authenticity and had a chef actually prepare real food instead of stage props. After the scene was finished we didn't want to let all the delicious food go to waste so everybody on the set, including the camera crew, had a big meal. Unfortunately, under the hot lights, some of the cream-filled pastries had become tainted and we all came down with a mild food poisoning. The picture was running over budget and the producer refused to halt production. I had to play my next love scene with a terrible stomach ache. The camera took a close-up of my face which was registering pain—and later the critics mistook the expression for one of love and raved about the emotion I'd put into the scene."

Warmed by the fire and entertained by his endless supply of stories, Katy felt relaxed and secure. She was no longer terrified of the black night and wilderness around them. The wild tides of passion had temporarily been dammed, and now she felt a comfortable, friendly companionship with Craig—one that made her love him even more. How nice it would be, she thought, to spend a lifetime with this exciting interesting man. She allowed her imagination to roam, daydreaming of how it would be to live with Craig, to know nights of blazing passion and utter fulfillment and then to lie quietly in the safety of his arms and enjoy his warm humor, his lust for draining every experience from life and savoring the memories.

But this would be the only night she would share with him, a poor counterfeit of the real thing. A silent tear trickled down her cheek, kept secret by the darkness.

At last she grew drowsy and fell asleep on the sand, close to the warm fire. Once during the night she awoke. The fire had been fed. She saw the outline of Craig's broad shoulders in the flickering light as he sat not far away, keeping watch. Reassured and secure, she fell asleep again, not waking until the light of dawn began filtering into the canyon.

Craig was poking at the coals of the fire with a fresh stick. "Didn't you sleep at all last night?" she asked.

He shrugged. "I dozed a few times. I don't require much sleep."

About mid-morning they heard the drone of an airplane motor. When it passed above them, they both waved. Craig had made a flag out of his shirt tied to a stick. The plane circled and came back. This time they saw a bundle come flying down through the air. It spashed into the river's edge close to the bank. Craig quickly waded out and retrieved it.

The bundle contained food and supplies and a note saying that a rescue party on inflatable rafts was on the way and should reach them in a few hours. The canyon was too narrow and the wind drafts too treacherous at this point to attempt a helicopter landing.

Their rescuers arrived shortly after noon. By nightfall they were back with the main group of the filming crew. The cot in Katy's tent felt like a king-size orthopedic mattress after sleeping on the damp river bank.

But Marsha was not about to allow her to go to sleep immediately. "The entire crew is buzzing with gossip and speculation. You've caused quite a stir, love, getting yourself stranded all night with Craig Sverenson for the second time. However do you manage to do that?"

"It wasn't my idea," Katy pointed out. "The canoe tipped over and I nearly drowned. There wasn't anything romantic about it. I was cold and miserable and scared half to death."

Marsha gave her a cynical look. "Are you sure about that?"

"Certainly," Katy said, avoiding her roommate's eyes.

"Well, you may have a bit of difficulty proving that to Dolores Ramon. I suppose you know she's livid with jealous fury. Careful or she'll scratch your eyes out next time she sees you."

Katy shrugged. "She doesn't have anything to be jealous about. Nothing happened between Craig and me. I know he's still in love with Dolores. I'm not going to mess my life up by getting into a hopeless romantic situation with a man who is still in love with his ex-wife. Craig doesn't love me." She hesitated. Then she said, "Tony's avoided me since we got back. I suppose he's thinking the worst of me, too."

"Well, you can hardly blame him for feeling a bit insecure and jealous. He wasn't too happy about your taking off on that canoe trip alone with Craig in the first place."

"I know," Katy sighed. "It was foolish of me to do

that. I frankly don't know how I let myself get into that situation. I should have just said 'no,' when Craig suggested it. Well," she remembered then, "I guess I did say no, but somehow I wound up going with Craig anyway. D'you suppose Tony will forgive me?"

"Oh, I think he will, if you explain the situation and reassure him that you and Craig didn't—well, you know, that you're still saving yourself for Tony." The English girl raised an eyebrow as she shot Katy a teasing look. "You *are* saving yourself for Tony, I assume?"

Katy blushed. "Of course. I'm not going to do anything to hurt Tony. He's too nice a guy. I'll tell him the truth—that Craig is not in love with me, and I'm not about to have an affair with a man who's in love with another woman. Tony will believe me."

She had a long talk with the magazine photographer the next day, and Tony did believe her. She was glad to see the look of relief and trust come back into Tony's eyes. She was truly fond of Tony. He believed she was a decent girl with self-respect. She assured him she had not traded that image for a shabby one-night stand on a river bank just to satisfy the physical need of a man who loved somebody else.

The film production spent the better part of a week on the river in the Big Bend country. Then they moved down the river to Laredo, one of the colorful cities on the Texas-Mexican border.

Once again, much to everyone's relief, they were out of tents, trailers and motor homes and into comfortable motel rooms. Katy spent an hour in the motel tub, soaking in a luxurious bubble bath. She was wrapped in a bath towel, seated before a vanity mirror when

Marsha cane in after having lunch with someone from the film crew.

"Guess what," Marsha announced. "It's party time again. Craig has sent word around that we're suspending production for a couple of days while everyone has some much needed 'R and R'—'Rest and Relaxation.' This afternoon some of us are going to a bullfight over in *Nuevo Laredo* on the Mexican side of the river. The star attraction is one of Mexico's most famous matadors, Roldolfo Belmondo Cortez de Cordoba." She paused for breath. "I think I got it right. And you probably won't be surprised to hear that he and Craig are old friends. Craig has reserved a *cantina* in *Nuevo Laredo* for a huge party tonight. He's even hired a band of *mariachis* to furnish the music."

"Sounds like fun."

"Oh, it will be. Craig's parties are always fun. Except—" Marsha hesitated "—Dolores Ramon has spread word around that she's going to make an important announcement at the party tonight. . . ."

Katy felt her cheeks grow pale.

Chapter Nine

That morning Katy crossed the International Bridge over the Rio Grande and went on a shopping expedition in Old Mexico. She was tired of looking like a river rat, tired of blue jeans and shirts. Her morale needed a boost for tonight's party when she might be seeing Craig for the last time. She knew she might find that morale in a new dress.

The party was to be held in a Mexican *cantina* with Mexican music, with the guest of honor a famous matador. Very well, Katy thought, she would dress accordingly. She would find a gown in the style of this land south of the border.

She wandered through the marketplace and then down narrow streets. At last, in a tiny shop window, she saw the perfect dress.

It had been hand sewn, created with loving skill by the elderly widow and her daughter who operated the shop. Katy asked in her halting high school Spanish to try the dress on. When she stood before a mirror she instantly fell in love with the exquisite gown.

It was a traditional Mexican dress of white lace. The heart-shaped neckline revealed her ample breasts bulging against a delicate lace bodice. The waistline tucked tightly around her middle. A full skirt covered with layer upon layer of wide ruffles fringed with red and black lace reached to her mid-calf. Long, lacy sleeves ended in double ruffles edged with red and black lace at the wrist cuffs. The shoes she tried on with the dress were designed in white "T"-strap fashion with heels designed to click crisply when stomped on the dance floor.

"Ah, mira! Que' bonita!" exclaimed the shop owner, clasping her hands excitedly as she moved around Katy, admiring the effect of the dress on the red-haired blue-eyed girl.

Then the older woman rattled a barrage of rapid-fire orders to her daughter who scurried to the back of the shop, quickly returning with a red rose and a mantilla.

Cooing soft endearments in Spanish, the shopkeeper showed Katy how to wear the rose in the left side of her hair. The white, triangular-shaped *mantilla*, held to her crown with a large, decorative comb, trailed down her back like a bridal veil.

Tears came to the eyes of the shop owner. *"Sēnorita,"* she said in broken English, "I sew these dress with love in my heart, just for one as beautiful as you."

Katy was filled with an emotion she couldn't explain as she viewed her image in the full length mirror. Why had she chosen this particular dress? It cast a strange emotional spell over her. Was it enchanted? She only knew she must have it. And she must wear it tonight.

The dress required only minor alteration around the

hem and waist. The shop owner assured her it could be done by tonight. Impulsively Katy told her she would buy it before even asking the price. When the cost was discussed, she was pleasantly surprised at how reasonably she could buy the dress considering the long hours of painstaking handwork that had gone into it.

Katy left the dress shop and had a traditional Mexican border town lunch. The waiters were polite and attentive, but it was an unhurried event, taking more than an hour from the time she gave the order until it was served and she had finished. She had a delicious guacamole salad, then a main course of refried beans, cabrito, chalupas, all topped off with mango ice cream.

Life here, she discovered, moved at a slower more genteel pace than in her hectic Manhattan. No one appeared to be in a rush. Inventing a flowery compliment for a woman was more important to the Latin men than getting somewhere on time.

She spent another hour wandering through souvenir shops, then hired a taxi to take her to *la corrida,* the bullfight ring, where she was to meet Marsha and Tony.

Tony, as usual, was well equipped with cameras. "We've been invited to join Craig Sverenson where the matadors dress," Tony told her as soon as she arrived.

"Yes, it's quite an honor," Marsha said, obviously excited. "Only VIP's and special friends of the matador are allowed there."

"How did you manage the invitation?" Katy asked curiously.

"I explained to Craig that I would like to have some pictures of him with his matador friend," Tony said. "Rodolfo de Cordoba is one of the world's great matadors, you know."

"No," Katy admitted. "I'm afraid I'm not up on matadors."

"Well, anyway, he is. In Latin countries a matador can be as famous as a movie superstar in our culture. *Personality Magazine* really should do a piece on this guy. He's famous in Spain, Mexico and South America."

"I'll talk to Mike about it," Katy said.

Tony led the way. It appeared to Katy that he had already made himself familiar with the arena and with the protocol of the event. He knew exactly where to go. With high school Spanish only slightly better than hers, he spoke to officials and police guards and presently they were walking down a tiled hallway and entered a large room where a flurry of excitement was taking place.

There was Craig, as usual a head taller than most of the men around him. He was talking with a handsome Latin man, obviously the matador. They were chatting in Spanish and laughing. Craig appeared to be as comfortable with the Spanish language as he was with English.

Then Craig spied them and motioned for them to join him. Switching to English, he introduced them. "These are my friends, Rodolfo. Miss Katy O'Hara from New York, a writer for *Personality Magazine*, Marsha Trident from Liverpool, my make-up lady and Tony Wilkins also from *Personality Magazine*, a very fine photographer whom I'd like to hire away from his present job. And this, my friends, is Rodolfo Belmondo Cortez de Cordoba, the world's greatest matador."

The bullfighter bowed, kissing Katy's and Marsha's hands in continental fashion. "How exquisitely beautiful you are," he said in perfect English. "Surely having such lovely and charming young ladies visit me will bring me great luck when I face *el toro* this afternoon."

Then he shook hands warmly with Tony. "If you are Craig's friend, then you are my friend, too." He laughed, flashing white teeth against a swarthy complexion. He put his arm around Craig in the effusive, emotional manner of Latin men. "Craig is more than a friend; he is like my own brother for many, many years. Have you told them, my friend, of the *encierro*, when we ran through the narrow streets of Pamplona in Spain, chased by the angry bulls? No. Well, it is a fine story, and you must tell Miss O'Hara for her magazine. We were very young then—two foolish young men made brave on Spanish wine."

Tony snapped some candid pictures of Craig and Rodolfo, then they wished him well in today's fights and departed.

Out in the hallway Marsha gasped. "That has to be the handsomest man I have ever met."

Katy smiled. "You're just a sucker for Latin charm."

"Oh, am I ever! I just love the beautiful way they flatter women."

"Surely you don't believe them," Katy laughed. "It's only a line. They gauge their macho on how well they can flatter a woman."

"I know—but I like it anyway."

Yes, Katy thought, Rodolfo was indeed a handsome man. But she'd only been able to see Craig. Would it be this way the rest of her life—measuring every man she met against Craig and having them come off second best?"

They went to the stands, Craig having arranged seats in the shade for the movie cast and film crew. Katy sat through the colorful parade through the arena which marked the start of the bullfights. But she had no stomach to sit through the bloody spectacle of the actual bullfight. She left the arena and caught a taxi which took her back to the dress shop. The alterations had been made. She tried the dress on again, then the shop owner placed it in a box for her.

Katy returned to the motel on the American side of the river. She napped most of the afternoon, waking when Marsha returned.

"How were the bullfights?" she asked drowsily.

"Bloody, but exciting. I've been to Spain several times, so this wasn't my initiation to the sport. I rather like it, in fact. I can see why it is so popular in Latin countries—the pageantry and all, the fundamental conflict between man and beast, life and death. Very basic. Very gutsy."

"How did your matador do?"

"Well, he isn't *my* matador, unfortunately, though I'll confess I certainly wish he were. But to answer your question, he did very well, indeed. Craig might have been stretching it a bit when he said Rodolfo was the world's greatest, but he's certainly up there with the best. Very polished and smooth. Takes hair-raising chances. The crowd loves him."

Then Marsha asked, "Aren't you going to get ready for the party?"

"I'll join you a little later," Katy replied. "I feel lazy today. I want to nap a bit more."

That was a small prevarication. For some reason that she couldn't explain, she didn't want Marsha to see her new dress until she made her entrance at the party. She felt curiously shy about it.

Marsha took a shower, dressed and left. Only then did Katy get up. She took a leisurely bath, then spent a lengthy time getting her make-up right. She was feeling feminine and pampered again after the rigors of the trip they had made down the river. At last she slipped into her dress, fitted the rose in her hair and the mantilla and comb as the shopowner had instructed. She gazed at the mirror and held her breath. The effect was even more than she'd hoped.

From the motel she took a taxi to the international bridge. On the other side she transferred to a Mexican cab which drove through the narrow streets of the border town in Old Mexico and stopped before the *Cantina del Mundo.*

When Katy stepped out of the cab she could hear the strains of the *mariachi* band inside, the clinking of glasses and the hum of many voices. The party was evidently in full swing. For weeks everyone had been under a strain, pressured by Craig's demand for perfection. Now it was time to relax and have fun. There would be laughter and songs and the tequila would flow like the river.

Katy paid the cab driver, crossed the narrow sidewalk. She stood before the *cantina* door for a moment, gathering her courage, then walked in.

For a moment she was swamped by the tide of humanity crowded into the party room of the bar. The sound of revelry was almost deafening. Then some of the noise died down. Katy became aware of heads turning, of eyes swinging in her direction. She realized she was making an entrance that brought the party to a brief surprised hush. She felt self-conscious, yet proud.

They were all looking at her—Tony, Marsha, Rodolfo, Dolores Ramon and Craig. Especially Craig. She saw the look of surprise and admiration in his eyes and a warm glow spread over her. This might be the last night he would ever see her. She wanted to leave him with a good memory of her.

She heard murmured exclamations of compliments on her dress around her. Marsha moved through the crowd and clasped her hand. "Katy, you are absolutely stunning!" she gasped. "Whenever did you get that dress?"

"This morning. Do you like it?"

"Do I like it? It's ravishing. You look like a bride . . . a lovely Spanish bride."

"A—a bride?" Katy echoed, reacting with a peculiar emotional shock.

Of course. The white lace. The *mantilla*. No wonder the dress had had such a magic effect on her from the moment she tried it on. Not until this moment was she consciously aware of the symbolism of the dress and the unconscious reason she had chosen it. It had struck a responsive chord deeply buried in her heart. It did make her look like a bride. That part of her that wanted to be Craig's bride had responded. The dress *was* enchanted—enchanted with her love for Craig. This was as close as she would ever come to being his bride, this last night with him, and the dress was the symbol of what might have been but could never be. . . .

Craig approached her. Quickly her heart reacted with a faster rhythm. "Well, Katy O'Hara," he said softly, taking her hand. "Is it really you?"

"Yes," she said unsteadily.

"What happened to the freckled little urchin in blue jeans and sneakers?"

"Did I look that bad?" she asked, her mouth feeling dry.

"Bad? No, I thought you looked adorable in your camping clothes." And in a low voice for only her ears, he made her cheeks burn by adding, "And even more adorable without them in the snowbound cabin that night. But tonight, in that dress—you are remarkably beautiful."

It was a moment of soaring elation for her heart. But the moment was bitterly short. For after the brief exchange he moved back in the crowd and then she saw him at the bar with Dolores. Their heads were together and she was holding his hand.

Dimly Katy realized Tony was at her side. She answered his compliments automatically. For her the pinnacle of the evening was over. She had made her entrance. She had seen Craig's eyes light up when he saw her. But it had only been the physical reaction of a man seeing an attractive woman. Now he was back with the woman he loved, Dolores Ramon, and for Katy the rest of the evening would be an empty charade as she forced herself to play her party role.

She spent time with Tony. Rodolpho Belmondo Cortez de Cordoba captured her for a while, maneuvering her into a private corner where he regaled her with Latin flattery that was sheer poetry and propositioned her in such a charming way she could only respond with an amused squeeze of his hand and a promise that if she ever decided to be seduced by a matador she'd be certain to place him at the head of the list.

Later in the evening Katy found herself face to face with Dolores Ramon. Katy was in the lounge of the women's restroom, repairing her make-up, when the glamorous Mexican movie star sat down in the chair at the vanity beside her. They were alone in the room.

"A lovely dress you have chosen for tonight, *señorita*," Dolores murmured smoothly. "Indeed, you look like a *señorita*. You dressed like that for Craig, am I correct?"

Katy blushed. "What gives you that idea?" she responded coldly.

Dolores shrugged. She pouted at the mirror as she touched her lips with make-up. "It is quite obvious.

One has only to see the way you look at Craig. I'm not blind, my dear. Furthermore I know that Craig is attracted to you—in a physical sort of way. I'm sure he would like to sleep with you. If he hasn't already—"

Katy felt her cheeks grow hot. "He certainly hasn't," she stammered. "I mean, we—"

Dolores glanced at her coolly. "You needn't protest. Your chastity is of no concern to me. Perhaps Craig did make love to you that night you were stranded on the river bank with him. I'd be surprised if he didn't. He's a strong virile man. The two of you alone all night. Well, what else would one expect of a man, especially when he's with a woman who is so obviously infatuated with him as you are?"

Katy said furiously, "I don't have to listen to any more of this."

She started to get up, but the Mexican movie star held her arm. "Please do listen. It's for your own good. Becoming romantically involved with Craig can only lead to disaster for you. Craig is my man, my husband. I'm going to prove that to you tonight. But even so, you cannot be safe from him. Craig can be irresistible. He may yet decide to have you, just to satisfy his male ego. Once Craig makes up his mind to conquer something—or someone—he usually succeeds. But consider the cost to yourself. In the end Craig will come back to me. He has a strong commitment to marriage, as you will see. So you might have a fling with him, but it would be no more than that. You would gain nothing but a broken heart. You are too young to wreck your life over such an impossible love. It would be better for you to forget about Craig Sverenson."

Katy drew a deep breath. Then she managed to keep her voice level. "Miss Ramon, let me assure you that I have already considered all those possibilities. I can also assure you that Craig has never made love to me, nor will he ever. It's true that I find Craig a very attractive man. Perhaps I have been infatuated with him. Yes, I'll admit that I have. But I have never let it get out of hand. I have completed my work on the article and I'm going to return to New York, probably tomorrow or the next day. I will never see Craig Sverenson again. He's all yours."

The look of smug triumph in Dolores Ramon's eyes galled her. But Katy swallowed her angry tears and fled from the room.

The party had become a disaster. She wanted only to leave. But before she could escape she had to endure a final heartbreak.

There was a fanfare from the band. Craig and his friend Rodolfo clambered up on the bar, helping Dolores to join them. Dolores held up her arms for attention. The sound of the revelry diminished. "My darling friends," she called out in her trained lyrical voice. "We have worked so hard on this film, *The Last Adventure*, together and this has been the most important film of my career, for it has brought Craig and me—together again. I want you all to know how happy I am. It's been an experience I won't soon forget."

A cheer and round of applause arose from the crowd.

Rodolfo de Cordoba then held up his arms for attention. When he could be heard, he added, "As you know, Craig is my good *amigo*. I want to invite all of you, the entire cast, all of the camera crew and technicians, the writers—everyone connected with this motion picture—to come to my ranch near Monterrey to be my guest for a big celebration for Dolores and Craig."

Then Craig and Dolores embraced and kissed. Katy saw them through a scalding curtain of tears.

She managed to slip quietly away from the party. She returned to the motel room. There she removed her lovely Mexican lace dress and carefully packed it away in the box.

She knew she would never wear it again.

Chapter Ten

The next day Katy phoned her editor at *Personality Magazine*. She gave him a brief summary of the material she had covered on Craig Sverenson, including the surprise announcement of his pending remarriage to Dolores Ramon. "Mike," she said, "I think at this point I have all the material I need for this article on Craig Sverenson and on his newest film. He'll be shooting a few final scenes in the next week or two, but I really can't see any point in my hanging around any longer. I'd be wasting my time and costing the magazine unnecessary expenses."

"All right, Katy," Mike Dale replied cheerfully. "I'll respect your judgment on that. But let's have Tony stay on down there a bit longer. I'd like for him to stick around till they shoot the final scenes. I want a good picture layout on this story."

Katy nodded, her heart leaden. "Yes, I'll tell him, Mike. And I'll get a plane out of here this afternoon."

Marsha Trident and Tony went with her to the airport. Katy hugged the English girl. "You've been a super roommate, Marsha. Gee, I'm going to miss you."

"And I you, love."

"If you're ever in New York, look me up. Promise?"

"Right. And the same goes for you if you're ever in Liverpool." Then Marsha said, "Are you certain you don't want to wait around until the next flight so you can tell Criag goodbye? He's going to be upset to hear you've left without even a farewell."

Katy shook her head. She tried to sound impersonal as she replied, "No, he's busy with the film and with Dolores. There's no point in my interrupting him. Just—just tell him goodbye for me. Tell him I appreciated his being so cooperative with the article I'm doing. And . . . thank him for rescuing me from the snow and fishing me out of the river. Tell him I—I guess he's right. I am just a city tenderfoot—"

She quickly turned away.

Tony walked with her to the boarding gate. They held hands. Katy kissed him. "I'll see you in New York in a few weeks, my friend."

"Count on it." Tony was sending her off with a cheerful grin. "Give my best to Mike and tell him I'm having a great time on his expense account."

"I'm sure he'll appreciate that!"

Katy was proud of the calm act she'd been able to pull off. But it dissolved once she was safely on board and out of Tony's and Marsha's eyesight. She huddled in her seat, her face turned to the window as tears ran down her cheeks. When the plane left the ground, she gazed down at the winding muddy ribbon, the Rio Grande. She had followed its course for hundreds of miles, from its birth as a tiny mountain stream near the

Continental Divide, almost to its mouth at the Gulf of Mexico. On its banks she had found a great love and a tragic heartbreak.

Back in New York Katy spent two days revising and polishing the final draft of her article and put it on Mike Dale's desk.

Later that day Mike called her into his office. "I've just finished reading your article," he mumbled around the stub of a cigar, scowling at her.

Katy's heart plummeted. "Is—is it that bad?"

"Bad? Hell, no, it's fantastic!"

Katy breathed a sigh of relief.

Mike went on, "It's a superlative job of in-depth reporting and writing. You did a sensitive study of Craig Sverenson's character and background. The descriptive passages of that trip down the Rio Grande are vivid. Makes me think I was on the scene, seeing everything. The anecdotal material is great for reader interest—those little incidents that happened to people in the camera crews, the rodeo episode, the story of how you were stranded in the canyon and Craig's survival skills—making a fire by rubbing a couple of sticks together, that kind of stuff. Katy, our readers are going to eat this stuff up. It's going to be a cover story, for sure."

Katy felt a warm response to Mike's praise. Yet with it her heart was sad. She wondered if she'd ever feel lighthearted again.

She became aware of Mike's penetrating gaze. "Seems to me," he said thoughtfully, "you left here despising Craig Sverenson. Said you didn't want to have anything to do with the man. Tried your best to get out of doing this assignment." He motioned at the manuscript on his desk. "I don't get that impression from reading your article. He comes through as a warm admirable human being—a bit egotistical and a trifle ruthless at times, a driving perfectionist . . . yet understandable. I gather that he's a bit of a showoff but also sensitive and intelligent. And you make a point that his macho image is not phony. He is a real adventurer, a daredevil who does most of his own dangerous film stunts himself. Sounds to me, Katy O'Hara, that you have done something of an about-face," Mike teased.

Katy was blushing furiously. "Well, I tried to be fair to him. . . ."

"Oh, you're fair, all right, as I knew you'd be. You're too good a reporter and too honest a writer to describe Craig Sverenson any way but what he's really like. I just wondered what made you change your mind?"

The conversation was becoming unbearably painful. "I—I just spent time getting to know him. He was not like I first thought. . . ."

"Well, you did a swell job, Katy. I expect your title of 'junior editor' is going to be changed to 'senior editor' very soon—with a boost in the old paycheck."

"Thank you, Mike." She tried to infuse a proper amount of enthusiasm in her voice. But somehow her response sounded hollow. The article was a success. Her career was a success. But was the price she'd paid too high? Was she doomed to feel this dull sadness in her heart forever?

Katy did her best to get a handle on her life again in the familiar surroundings of Manhattan. She had her lunches in the places where she was used to eating. She window-shopped the areas she liked, visited the used bookstalls, went to the museum and saw a play.

In the apartment she cleaned her closet, rearranged her room, changed her hair style.

This was the city where she'd lived all of her life. The apartment had been her home since she was a little girl.

Yet now she felt like a stranger who had been away a long, long time. At night, when she was going to sleep, she imagined she heard the murmur of the river close by. When she walked from her bus stop to her office, she looked up between the canyon walls of the sky-scrapers and thought that the sky wasn't blue as it should be.

She was able to fool the office staff but her father was more perceptive. Several times Katy caught him regarding her with an expression of concern. He was obviously aware of her unhappiness. But she knew he wouldn't intrude on her privacy unless she offered to talk first. And she couldn't bring herself to put her feelings into words. The hurt was too fresh, too poignant. Perhaps after a while she would be able to tell him.

Several times in the next weeks she caught sight of a tall, broad-shouldered man, a head above the rest of the crowd on a sidewalk and her heart gave a wrench at his resemblance to Craig. Once she passed a movie house showing one of Craig's old movies. Impulsively she went up to the box office to buy a ticket, then realized what she was doing and turned and fled.

She wondered if the hurt would be dulled enough for her to be able to see him in *The Last Adventure* when it was released. She didn't know how she could stay away after being so close to the filming of the movie and knowing how much the main character reflected the real Craig Sverenson. And yet, could she bear the fresh heartache of seeing him again, even on the screen?

The filming of *The Last Adventure* was completed. Tony Wilkins returned from his assignment. The first day he was back at the office he asked Katy for a dinner date that evening. He chose the same Greenwich

Village restaurant they had visited shortly before leaving on the Craig Sverenson assignment.

When they walked into the small family-operated establishment, Katy thought about all that had happened to her since they last ate here. It seemed a lifetime ago.

At a small corner table, over a bottle of wine, Tony told her how he had traveled down to Brownsville, Texas with the film crew and finally to the mouth of the Rio Grande for the final scenes of *The Last Adventure.*

Katy wanted most of all to hear about Craig, but the questions remained in her heart unspoken.

"Marsha sent her love," Tony said. "Said she missed sharing a tent with you."

Katy smiled. "Having Marsha for a tent-mate made the outdoor experience almost bearable."

"You still hate the outdoor life as much?"

She considered his question. "Y'know, Tony, I was sure I did. But strangely, since I've been back, the buildings seem to hem me in. The smog bothers me more. And the sky is definitely not as blue."

He grinned. "Guess you've been converted."

"Well, I never thought I'd admit it, but—"

He was looking at her thoughtfully. He suddenly reached across the table and put his hand on hers. "Katy, I'd hoped when we went off on that expedition that I was going to see a whole lot of you. We'd be thrown together in a romantic setting. I had planned to tell you—"

A tiny frown penciled her brow. She turned her palm up, lacing her fingers in his, giving them a squeeze. "Wait, Tony," she said huskily. "I'm afraid you're about to get serious on me. I have to tell you—"

He smiled ruefully. "No, I guess you don't have to

tell me, Katy," he interrupted. "I think I know the answer before I ask the question. I'm sure it wasn't just an accident that we really weren't together much on the trip. I'm sure if you'd really wanted to be with me all the time, you would have been."

Katy took a breath. "I'm sorry, Tony. You're the last person I'd ever want to hurt. I'm genuinely fond of you. But I'm not in love with you. I guess I didn't know that until we were on the expedition—because I didn't actually know what being in love was like. Now that I know, I just can't settle for less than that. I wouldn't be fair to myself and it certainly wouldn't be fair to you."

Tony looked at her for a long moment, then said, "It's Craig, isn't it?"

She swallowed hard and nodded, unable to speak.

"I kind of figured. I mean, Marsha talked with me quite a bit after you left. She was pretty sure you'd fallen in love with Craig."

"It was one-sided, Tony. Craig doesn't know how I feel. I never told him. And Tony, nothing happened between Craig and me. It was just one of those ridiculous one-way situations. I fell head-over-heels in love with the guy. He couldn't see me for sour apples— or rather, I should say, for the glamorous Dolores Ramon. Oh, I'm sure he would have enjoyed a fling with me, a temporary affair. I'm not going to settle for anything like that. When I say 'yes' to a man it's going to be with a fellah who loves me as much as I love him."

"Good for you. That's the way it should be." Then Tony shot her a wry smile. "Ironic, ain't it? The last time we had dinner here, you were telling me how much you hated Craig Sverenson and how you wished you didn't have to go on that assignment."

She nodded. "I lived to eat my words," she admitted.

"By the way, you might like to know that after the picture was completed, Craig dropped the charges against that has-been actor, Ronnie Crowder. I know you were pretty worked up over that situation and I thought you'd like to know the outcome."

"Yes, I was and I'm glad you told me. Marsha once told me that in spite of what a slave driver Craig could be at times, he wasn't as mean as his bite. Craig felt only scorn for Ronnie who I thought was a tragic case. I'm glad Craig isn't going to be vindictive and send him to jail for a long time."

They fell silent as the waiter served their meal. Then as they started eating Tony surprised her by saying casually, "By the way, you won't be seeing me at the magazine anymore."

She put her fork down, staring at him. "What do you mean?"

"Well, Craig and I got to be pretty good friends. My camera work impressed him, especially after he found out I know a lot about underwater photography. He's offered me a good job with a camera crew he's taking to the Caribbean for his next location job."

"That is a shocker," Katy said slowly. "We'll miss you. *I'll* miss you. I hope you're not leaving because of me—because we couldn't get together—"

"Oh, I might have stayed around here if I thought there was a chance for things working out for you and me. But to tell the truth, I really want this job. The pay is good and it's something I definitely want to do."

"Then I'm glad for you, Tony."

The weeks of summer slipped by. Early autumn brought a spell of heavy rains to Manhattan. Katy left her office late one afternoon. Outside, the rain-slick streets were growing dark. She stood in the doorway of her office building, preparing to open her umbrella, thinking that the weather suited her dismal mood.

The door of a cab opened. A large man stepped out and crossed the sidewalk in two giant strides. He slipped his hand under her arm. "Come on," he said. "I have a cab waiting."

Katy stared up at Craig Sverenson. The patter of rain, the rumble of traffic became a blur in her ears. She felt stunned. Her mind was paralyzed.

Vaguely she was aware of his strong arm guiding her across the crowded sidewalk. Then they were in the taxi. Craig said something to the driver.

Katy went on staring up at Craig. His deeply tanned face contrasted with the city pallor she was familiar with on the people she saw every day. His head was bare. Drops of rain clung to his thick, dark hair. His eyes were the same forest green flecked with brown that she remembered so vividly.

She opened her mouth twice before she was able to speak. Then all she could manage to say was, "What are you doing here?"

He smiled, reminding her how even and white his teeth were against his weathered complexion. "Why, I came to see you."

The shock, the numbness had not yet worn off. She blinked like a somnambulist. Surely she was dreaming. Had she dozed off at her desk? Surreptitiously, she fumbled under her rain coat, pinched her leg and determined that she was, indeed, awake.

Her thinking processes were gradually accepting the reality of this impossible development. She was actually sitting in a New York taxicab with Craig Sverenson. It was happening. She shook her head slowly, dazed and unbelieving.

"I don't understand—"

"It's quite simple. I came to see you. I would have come much sooner, but I've been swamped with wrapping up the picture, the final scenes, and I wanted to have some say in the cutting. The sound had to be dubbed—"

She looked at him blankly, not comprehending his words. "I'm—I'm sorry," she mumbled. "But I'm in a state of shock. What did you say?"

"Never mind. Here, driver," he called.

He opened the door. She was aware of him paying the driver, guiding her across another sidewalk into a small quiet cafe, where he led her to a secluded booth.

"That rain is chilly. Would you like something to warm you . . . a hot rum drink, perhaps?"

She remembered her experience with hot buttered rum that first day she met Marsha Trident in the Colorado ski lodge. "No thank you. A hot chocolate will be fine."

The waiter brought their drinks. Craig was smiling at her. She was doing her best to cope with her tumultuous emotions. Questions were rattling around in her brain like ricocheting bullets. Again she shook her head. "I just don't understand."

"Well, we're going to premiere *The Last Adventure* in California. I want you to be at the premiere with me."

She stared at him. Had he taken leave of his senses?

"By the way," he said, "I saw the current issue of *Personality Magazine* with your article about me and about the film. It was quite good. You're a fine writer, Katy O'Hara."

"Wait a minute," she said in a befuddled voice. "You're talking too fast. Go back to what you said before that."

"About the premiere? Yes, I want you to be there with me. That's why I came here to New York. To take you back with me."

A frown penciled her brow. For the first time a definite emotion—anger—emerged from the storm inside her. "I should think your wife would take a dim view of an arrangement like that!"

"Perhaps she would, if I had a wife. Which I do not."

"But—but you and Dolores—" she gasped.

"—are *not* married," he concluded.

"Not married?" A tiny glimmer of hope stirred in a spot of her heart that had been empty for so long.

"Yes. Dolores was up to her old tricks again," he said with a note of sadness. "This time it was with the matador, Rodolfo de Cordoba. I caught them together."

"But he was supposed to be such a great friend. He said you were like brothers."

"Yes, well I guess he wasn't such a good friend," Craig smiled wryly. "Rodolfo never allowed a friendship to interfere with a romantic conquest. But I can't blame him. Dolores is a blindingly beautiful woman, at least on the surface. When she goes after a man, it isn't easy for him to refuse. Rodolfo is only human . . . as all the others were."

He reached across the table, captured her hands in his powerful grip, looked straight into her eyes. "Katy O'Hara, I want to explain something to you. I was in love with Dolores, very much, at one time, when we were first married. I suppose in a certain way, a part of that love will remain with me. When one divorces, severs ties with a person he or she once loved, a residue of those old memories and emotions remain. But I am no longer *in* love with Dolores. Believe me on that score. Nevertheless, I am very idealistic about marriage. I am not like so many Hollywood actors you read about who go casually from one marriage into another. Marriage to me is a serious matter. My early family conditioning and my religious beliefs give me a strong conviction about marriage being a permanent relationship. So when Dolores came back to do the film with me, said she had reformed and begged for another chance to try and make our marriage work, I felt morally obligated to give her another chance—to give our marriage another chance."

He paused, carefully searching for the right words. "I was having a conflict over the situation," he explained, "because I was so attracted to you from the first moment I picked you up out of the snow. I tried not to admit to myself for a while that I was falling in love with you. But you seemed to dislike me so much at first. Then I saw you kiss Tony Wilkins in the pueblo that night in New Mexico. And later, when we were stranded on the river bank, you said you and Tony were probably going to be married when you returned to New York—"

The glimmer of hope began to spread into a tremendous golden glow radiating from her heart throughout her being. "Did—did you say something about thinking you were in love with me?" she whispered.

"Yes," he nodded, capturing and holding her eyes with his intense gaze. "I was falling in love with you . . . I *am* in love with you, Katy. And you are in love with me."

The glow had burst into a joyous song within her. Her eyes were bright, her bosom was rising and falling swiftly. "Now just wait a minute, Craig Sverenson. You and your male ego! What makes you so sure I love you?"

"Because," he replied, his eyes twinkling, "Tony

Wilkins told me. As you know, he resigned from *Personality Magazine* and accepted a job I offered him. When he came back from New York, he got me aside and had a long talk with me. Told me that he'd as good as proposed to you but you turned him down because you'd fallen in love with me."

Katy blushed as she sent a thought wave of gratitude to good old Tony.

"Well," Craig demanded, "was Tony right? Do you love me, Katy O'Hara?"

"That all depends. What do you have in mind?"

"I have in mind marrying you, my girl. I love you. I want you for my wife. Shall I get down on one knee here in this cafe and make it a formal proposal?"

"That would be nice," she smiled with a feeling that the clouds had parted above her and a heavenly chorus was filling the air with a glorious hymn of joy. "Or you could just kiss me."

He moved to her side of the booth and obliged her. It was a long kiss. When it ended, he said, holding her tightly, "I loved that dress you wore the last night I saw you in Mexico. Do you think it could be your wedding dress?"

"Yes," she said breathlessly. "And here I thought I'd never wear that dress again!"

IT'S YOUR OWN SPECIAL TIME

Contemporary romances for today's women.
Each month, six very special love stories will be yours
from SILHOUETTE.
Look for them wherever books are sold
or order now from the coupon below.

$1.50 each

Silhouette Romance

___#55 WINTER'S HEART Ladame   ___#77 SECRET MARRIAGE Cork

___#56 RISING STAR Trent   ___#78 DOUBLE OR NOTHING Oliver

___#57 TO TRUST TOMORROW John   ___#79 TO START AGAIN Halldorson

___#58 LONG WINTER'S NIGHT Stanford   ___#80 WONDER AND WILD DESIRE Stephens

___#59 KISSED BY MOONLIGHT Vernon   ___#81 IRISH THOROUGHBRED Roberts

___#60 GREEN PARADISE Hill   ___#82 THE HOSTAGE BRIDE Dailey

___#61 WHISPER MY NAME Michaels   ___#83 LOVE LEGACY Halston

___#62 STAND-IN BRIDE Halston   ___#84 VEIL OF GOLD Vitek

___#63 SNOWFLAKES IN THE SUN Brent   ___#85 OUTBACK SUMMER John

___#64 SHADOW OF APOLLO Hampson   ___#86 THE MOTH AND THE FLAME Adams

___#65 A TOUCH OF MAGIC Hunter   ___#87 BEYOND TOMORROW Michaels

___#66 PROMISES FROM THE PAST Vitek   ___#88 AND THEN CAME DAWN Stanford

___#67 ISLAND CONQUEST Hastings   ___#89 A PASSIONATE BUSINESS James

___#68 THE MARRIAGE BARGAIN Scott   ___#90 WILD LADY Major

___#69 WEST OF THE MOON St. George   ___#91 WRITTEN IN THE STARS Hunter

___#70 MADE FOR EACH OTHER Afton Bonds   ___#92 DESERT DEVIL McKay

___#71 A SECOND CHANCE ON LOVE Ripy   ___#93 EAST OF TODAY Browning

___#72 ANGRY LOVER Beckman   ___#94 ENCHANTMENT Hampson

___#73 WREN OF PARADISE Browning   ___#95 FOURTEEN KARAT BEAUTY Wisdom

___#74 WINTER DREAMS Trent   ___#96 LOVE'S TREACHEROUS JOURNEY Beckman

___#75 DIVIDE THE WIND Carroll   ___#97 WANDERER'S DREAM Clay

___#76 BURNING MEMORIES Hardy   ___#98 MIDNIGHT WINE St. George

   ___#99 TO HAVE, TO HOLD Camp

- -

SILHOUETTE BOOKS, Department SB/1
1230 Avenue of the Americas
New York, NY 10020

Please send me the books I have checked above. I am enclosing
$_____ (please add 50¢ to cover postage and handling. NYS and
NYC residents please add appropriate sales tax). Send check or
money order—no cash or C.O.D.'s please. Allow six weeks for delivery.

NAME_____

ADDRESS_____

CITY_____ STATE/ZIP_____

15-Day Free Trial Offer
6 Silhouette Romances

6 Silhouette Romances, free for 15 days! We'll send you 6 new Silhouette Romances to keep for 15 days, absolutely free! If you decide not to keep them, send them back to us. You pay nothing.

Free Home Delivery. But if you enjoy them as much as we think you will, keep them by paying us the retail price of just $1.50 each. We'll pay all shipping and handling charges. You'll then automatically become a member of the Silhouette Book Club, and will receive 6 more new Silhouette Romances every month and a bill for $9.00. That's the same price you'd pay in the store, but you get the convenience of home delivery.

Read every book we publish. The Silhouette Book Club is the way to make sure you'll be able to receive every new romance we publish.

This offer expires January 31, 1982

READERS' COMMENTS ON SILHOUETTE ROMANCES:

"Your books are written with so much feeling and quality that they make you feel as if you are part of the story."

—D.C.*, Piedmont, SC

"I'm very particular about the types of romances I read; yours more than fill my thirst for reading."

—C.D., Oxford, MI

"I hope Silhouette novels stay around for many years to come. . . . Keep up the good work."

—P.C., Frederick, MD

"What a relief to be able to escape in a well-written romantic story."

—E.N.. Santa Maria, CA

"Silhouette Romances . . . Fantastic!"

—M.D., Bell, CA

"I'm pleased to be adding your books to my collection—my library is growing in size every day."

—B.L., La Crescenta, CA

* Names available on request.